THE GONE DEAD

ALSO BY CHANELLE BENZ

The Man Who Shot Out My Eye Is Dead

THE GONE DEAD

A Novel

WITHDRAWN

CHANELLE BENZ

ecco

An Imprint of HarperCollinsPublishers

THE GONE DEAD. Copyright © 2019 by Chanelle Benz. All rights reserved. Printed in the United States of America. No part of this book may be used or reproduced in any manner whatsoever without written permission except in the case of brief quotations embodied in critical articles and reviews. For information, address HarperCollins Publishers, 195 Broadway, New York, NY 10007.

HarperCollins books may be purchased for educational, business, or sales promotional use. For information, please e-mail the Special Markets Department at SPsales@harpercollins.com.

FIRST EDITION

Designed by Renata De Oliveira

Library of Congress Cataloging-in-Publication Data

Names: Benz, Chanelle, author.
Title: The gone dead : a novel / Chanelle Benz.
Description: New York : Ecco, [2019]
Identifiers: LCCN 2018036322 | ISBN 9780062490698
Classification: LCC PS3602.E7248 G66 2019 | DDC 813/.6—dc23
LC record available at https://lccn.loc.gov/2018036322

ISBN 978-0-06-249069-8

19 20 21 22 23 LSC 10 9 8 7 6 5 4 3 2 1

. . . che quanto piace al mondo è breve sogno

—PETRARCH

Hang yourself, poet, in your own words. Otherwise, you are dead.

—LANGSTON HUGHES

THE GONE DEAD

BILLIE
2003

IT IS NOT EXACTLY AS SHE WAS PICTURING. THE HOUSE WHERE HER father once lived. But she remembers it or feels like she does. She puts the car back in gear and turns off the main road, bumping down the gravel drive toward it.

Billie parks and Rufus pops up in the back, his head veering between the driver and passenger seats, nosing her arm. Her hands stretch across the top of the wheel, palms thick and tingling from the long drive. She gets out and opens the back door. The dog bounds to the front porch, sniffs, and pees on the corner of the battered wooden steps.

"Thanks," she says as he gallops across the overgrown yard.

Her father's house squats above the ground on concrete blocks, its chipped wooden boards holding on for dear life to flaking white paint. There are two front doors and two front windows, a sloping screenless porch, and a rusting tin roof. She takes out the key her uncle sent and unlocks the door on the right, walking into a living room littered with broken chunks of filthy tile and the corpse of a brown carpet. There's a fireplace on her left with a broken space heater inside and an old Christmas bow hanging off the mantel. The planks of the ceiling are mismatched and one has even fallen halfway loose in the middle of the room, but the doorframes look new and the air is sweet with the smell of fresh-cut wood, her uncle's doing.

She walks into her father's bedroom. Or his thirty years ago. In the dust over the mirror above the mantel, she traces the ghost of her face, then walks the circumference of the room, a hand dragging along the wall. What of him is there in the spattered remains of floral wallpaper? Can she absorb it? Is it drawn to her skin?

The second door in the bedroom takes her into the back of the house, where the light is weak and the ceiling low. This is where she slept when she visited. Her father put the card table on the front porch and set up her cot with the purple-pink sheets. But she would sneak into his bed when she got scared. Even if Daddy wasn't there.

A trail of old newspapers and dead crickets leads her into the kitchen. The back wall of the house is in bad shape, buckling like the sides of a sunken ship. There's a pair of torn curtains in the sink. Looks like her uncle definitely didn't get around to cleaning. She unlocks the back door and steps onto a small, raised porch without a railing. Rufus is shopping a collection of perished things for something to chew:

old tires, a love seat, a broken fan, bloated bits of cardboard used to cover the windows during winter.

"Rufus, come."

He turns and trots into the woods behind the house. Dammit. It was probably unwise to let him off leash.

"Stay out of the road!" says the woman who hasn't owned a living thing since a goldfish called Nameles, which took three days to float to the top of its bowl. She was ten and her mother had been studying medieval hunting guides.

Billie sits on the porch and stretches her legs across the wood, trying to touch her toes. It's still freezing back home in Philly. The guy at the local gas station said it would get cold tonight. A cold snap he called it. She closes her eyes, turning her face toward the dogged southern sun, almost melting into sleep.

She had forgotten about this house, figured it'd been knocked down forever ago. But apparently it had been waiting for her: passing from her father to her mother, then to her mother's mother, and now that Gran has passed, to her. It's all she owns until she's done making payments on the car.

Inside, she rolls up the old carpet, tossing it into the backyard, then she sweeps and wipes down every surface. It gets holy—the scratch of the broom, the T-shirt stuck to the bottom of her back, the raw corners of her fingers beginning to bleed. The rain wakes her from her trance and she goes onto the front porch, where Rufus is gnashing the vines curling off the side of the house. He looks at her, then bounds up the porch steps.

She bends to stroke his dark wet head. "Am I going to

become one of those people who talks too much to their pet?"

He used to be Gran's. Billie has gotten this dog, this shack, and five thousand dollars from her grandmother, a woman she barely knew because even after her mother died, she always spent holidays with her mother's best friend, Jude.

The dog follows her into the bedroom, where she dries his paws with the towel from the backseat of the car. She tosses it in the corner and strips off her shirt. Nobody will see—two trucks have driven by here in the last three hours. She drags her suitcase to the bedroom closet, the only one in the house. There's a calendar on the top shelf, the Kennedy brothers dreamed onto a defiantly serene MLK. JFK looks somber and regal, but Robert Kennedy looks so sad he might cry, his eyes an unreal Caribbean blue. She hangs it up on an old nail left in the middle of the living room wall.

Hurrying before it gets dark, Billie takes a fading trail to the creek that runs through the woods behind the house. Rufus circles her, diving in and out of the brush. At the bank, the muddy water crashes slowly into itself. Behind her, the sun is scarring the sky pink, turning the tops of the trees black.

Her cousins tried to teach her to fish in this creek. They teased her when she wouldn't get in because soft things were always gliding by—that and the feel of mud moving between her toes like it was alive. But they always let her tag along, even though she was the baby and everyone said she was spoiled.

The dog barks from somewhere. "Rufus?" She pulls a handful of treats from her pocket. "Rufus, come!" She waits but he doesn't reappear. It is dark when she walks back, keeping an eye out for poison ivy, even though she doesn't remember what it looks like.

At the house, all of the lights are out. She stops, then walks around to the front. The driveway is empty except for her car. The flat blue fields along the main road are still. She knows she left at least one light on—the porch, the living room, something—and her uncle said he'd be working. The damn dog is nowhere to be seen. She slips the keys between her fingers for potential gouging. It could be nothing. Maybe the wiring is so old that a fuse blew.

She kicks the mud off the heels of her combat boots and rushes up the porch, unlocking the door and throwing it open so that it slams the wall behind. She waits. Nothing in the night but frogs and ghosts. Her ghosts. She walks through the house deliberately measured, snapping on every light.

In the bedroom, her wallet is still on top of the sweatpants she wore to clean the house. So, if someone did come in, they just turned off the lights. Unless she turned off the lights. She must've turned off the lights.

She unzips her suitcase and takes the gun out of a men's white sock. She checks the safety and tucks it in the back of her pants. All right, cowboy, that's pretty uncomfortable. She takes it out and stuffs it back in the sock. She's being silly. It's just an old house. Except for temporarily losing the dog to the Delta, everything is fine, right? But she takes the sock into the living room, where she pulls off her boots, putting them on the mantel to dry despite there being no source of heat. The guy at the gas station was right, it's getting chilly.

She grabs a sweatshirt and unfolds the plastic deck chair she brought and sits. Rufus strolls through the open door.

"Where the hell have you been?"

He flops down at her feet. She brushes the grass off his back and shuts the door. Something falls outside. Rufus barks, and she jumps. "Jesus! We both need to get used to noises, okay?"

Half an hour later, wrapped in her sleeping bag, cold but feeling brave, Billie drags the plastic chair onto the porch and sets the gun sock underneath. Rufus follows. "You can only come out if you lie down." He jumps off the porch. "For fuck's sake." He jumps back up. "C'mon, dog, give a girl a break."

In the field across the road is what's left of a barn. One night in southern Utah, she went camping with her mom and Jude in a ghost town. It had been a railroad town until the trains stopped coming through. Its roofless buildings and rusting cars seemed to be waiting for someone to tell them that they could stop holding on, that no one was coming back, that they could give in to that sweet final collapse.

She's missed traveling. After her father left them to become a bachelor poet, they moved to London for a year, then New Orleans, then to a shared apartment in Boston while her mother got her degrees, and in between they stayed with Jude in Utah, camped, or slept in the back of their blue pickup truck, the one with the white stripe and bad transmission. Sometimes her mother homeschooled her or sometimes she was enrolled in a school where new friends would say: Is that your mom? She's so young. She's so pretty. She doesn't look like you. And new bullies would say: Is your dad black? Like black was a bad dirty thing. And her mother would say: They're just jealous. You are beautiful. Like moms do.

Billie never knew that they were struggling because poor meant hungry and she was never hungry; she didn't know her beloved bike or clothes came from the Salvation Army. She thought her erudite mother just didn't believe in cable TV, or the Brownies, or the beauty of Leif Garrett, not that they didn't have the money. Then finally her mother landed a job as a medievalist in Philly and Billie started at Temple University, and one month into her freshman year they found out what the bleeding meant. Her mother was sick. *Work, work now, oh dearly beloved, work all that thou canst. For thou knowest not when thou shalt die, nor what shall happen unto thee after death.* Her mother taped these words to the wall above her desk.

Her phone rings.

"You settling in all right?" It's her uncle, her father's younger brother. His voice is tired but melodic, like he's been singing too long.

"Yeah, thanks for setting up the electricity." She kicks at the herd of mosquitoes congregating above her ankles. "Hey, did you stop by?"

"When?"

"Today—tonight." She yanks the sleeping bag over her feet.

"Nope. I'm on the road."

"You don't think anyone would come out here to steal something, do you?"

"Someone out there bothering you?"

"No, it's— No, no one's out here." She pulls the sleeping bag to her chin. "I'm used to the city, I guess."

"You get you a gun like I told you?"

"Yeah, but it's not like I know how to use it." Wind chimes sound from a distant porch, though she can't see any other houses. Rufus sways up from the floor, creaking across the loose planks, and rests his soft black head on her toes.

"And let your water faucets drip tonight so the pipes don't freeze. I heard there's a frost on."

"I bought a handgun. Should I have bought a shotgun?"

"You planning on hunting?"

"No way." But maybe her uncle hunts. "I'm not saying I'm against it. If it's done properly." She waits, but he says nothing. "So, I'll see you when you get back in town?"

"You gonna come over Friday night, right?"

"Yes, of course. I'm looking forward to it. Okay, safe travels then."

But her uncle doesn't hang up. "There could be someone out there."

"Uncle Dee—what do you mean?"

"Drugs are a problem in Greendale cause they ain't no jobs. Gangs are everywhere nowadays. Could be some crackhead looking for something to sell."

"Well, I don't have anything. I don't even have a TV. I need a break from the news anyway." She decides against asking what he thinks of the Iraq war. It's a bit early in their relationship to get into politics.

"Now your closest neighbor is Jim McGee. If there's a problem, you go over and tell him you are Cliff's daughter. He'll scare off any suspicious characters."

"I don't know that anyone's actually out here. Also, wouldn't I call the police?"

He snorts. "Up to you." He takes a drag off of his cigarette. "It'd be good for Jim to know you out there."

"Who's Jim?"

"I told you, Jimmy McGee, he the closest house to you."

"I mean, is he anyone to me?"

"He knew your daddy." Her uncle covers the phone for a second, mumbling something to somebody. "At one time, the McGees owned all that land round there. We worked for them."

"Did you tell him I was coming?"

"Ain't spoken to Jim in twenty years."

"And you're sure he's the guy I want to go to?"

"They known our family a long time. He'll help you if there's trouble."

"I'm fine, really. I just got spooked."

She gets off the phone with her uncle, then takes the gun from under the chair. A stupid buy. The chances of her defending herself during a home invasion are statistically abysmal. But that night she sleeps with the dog and the sock by her bed.

LOLA

LOLA HAS COME DOWN FROM MEMPHIS TO VISIT NANA AND IT MUST BE fate. She is sitting on Nana's blue armchair, her favorite since she can remember, indulging in a can of Coke—she don't keep this sugary shit at home. Didn't she just have her teeth bleached? There goes $400. Cause it's cigarettes, Coke, and BBQ once she's back in the Delta. This is why her mother never comes back down here except for Christmas. Says it's small-minded and broken, and that everyone who could fix it leaves, herself included. But for Lola, the stillness of the fields, the folks out on their porches, Nana's crooked voice drowning out the radio, pretending like every black woman can sing, is love.

Lola swivels the chair to the small kitchen where Nana is cooking in her housecoat. "How long has Billie been here?"

Nana looks at her, a spatula in one hand. "Who told you that?"

"Junior."

"That boy can't keep a thing to himself." Nana turns the burner low and lifts the pan, pushing scrambled eggs onto a plate. "I was told she got in yesterday."

"And nobody gone to see her?"

"Nobody supposed to according to your cousin Dee."

"Why y'all listening to that joker?" Lola comes to the counter, taking her plate of bacon and eggs back to the blue chair. "What kind of family is Billie gonna think we are?"

Nana cracks another egg in the pan, turning the burner back up. "Dee has his reasons."

"You think that's what her daddy would want?"

"Child, the dead don't get what they want."

Lola picks out the most burned piece of bacon, then takes a bite of eggs. Only Nana's chickens lay them this fresh. "It don't sound like you, Nana, not to be welcoming somebody."

"Them folks always brought trouble on themselves and can't nobody help them out of it. That's the way your granddaddy's side is."

Maybe Nana doesn't have the energy to get involved. She's definitely moving slower this year. But where's the drama in saying hello?

"Your teeth look good, baby."

Lola smiles wide for her. "Thank you, Nana."

"Your young man pay for it?"

"Yeah." Lola puts her fork down.

"Pick up that bottom lip and finish your eggs."

"I'm full."

"Oh my goodness"—Nana turns back to the pan—

"there's nothing wrong with having a good man take care of you."

"It was a birthday present."

"A good man gives you walking-around money."

"You sound like something out of *The Godfather*." Lola puts her plate down on the TV tray. "I hate to think of Billie out there on her own."

"She's a grown woman. Let her make peace with her daddy's ghost and move on." Nana slips a fried egg onto a plate and turns off the stove, carrying the plate into the living room. "Get your behind up off my good chair."

Lola stands. "I'm gonna go get a Coke."

"What's wrong with the Coke in the fridge?"

"I drank it all."

LOLA WALKS DOWN THE BUSTED SIDEWALK, PICKING HER WAY through the glass and trash gnarled around weeds. A column of smoke is pouring up into the sky; somebody burning leaves. The street looks wild and broken. Maybe it was always this broken, but now it looks like it has given up. She goes to the corner store, where she can smoke. Nana still doesn't know. Doesn't think it's ladylike. Something she must have been told when she was a housekeeper for a rich white lady across the tracks because as far as Lola's concerned if you're black in the Delta you do whatever you can to make life sweet.

She leans against the side of the store and lights a cigarette. Back when she was a kid and came down to visit, people used to be out. They'd be playing tag and kickball while folks sat on their porches gossiping. Now the neighborhood looks like everybody left and a few survivors of whatever apocalypse wander out every once in a while down the middle of the road wearing backpacks carrying everything they own. Maybe it's foolish to want this place to be like it was, as if the past was better when as a kid she really just didn't know all that was going on. But back then there was no minimum mandatory, no crack, more jobs, and not one of her cousins was in jail. Her uncles say that back then you always had a little money in your pocket. Now they barely got money for gas and the nearest catfish farm is an hour-and-a-half drive. She takes a last drag, then puts her cigarette out on the wall and pockets it.

Inside, she wanders the tilted linoleum aisles where something is leaking and draining toward the front door. She steps over the thin brown stream and opens the refrigerator, taking out a two-liter of Coke. Behind the register is a framed photograph taken during a Mardi Gras parade, a black queen at the center, all tiara and white teeth. Bet she had braces and bleach, maybe even headgear. Or maybe that was just her.

It's only teeth her girlfriends say, that and her man is dead sexy. A phrase Lola can't stand. None of them grew up with a man pleaser like her mother. With a stepdaddy who would say this is my house and you are a guest in it. You eating off my plates, using up my hot water, everything in here you treat with respect or you will feel my hand. A mother who didn't say a damn thing, but just stood by, keeping her mouth shut, then comforted her afterward, when Lola couldn't sit down.

Whatever. What she needs to be focusing on is budgeting some kinda way. Yesterday she sent those evil-ass debt collectors a cease and desist letter to stop them from contacting her because they about to start threatening to break her legs. But the letter don't do a thing about the debt. When they told her that they wanted five thousand, she almost laughed because they might as well have said five hundred thousand.

Q: What does it mean that she, her family's first college graduate, is living off of pasta and (sometimes dry) cereal so she can afford gas and rent?
A: *That she will pay interest for the rest of her life without ever touching the damn principal.*

Back out in Greendale or Baghdad or wherever, Lola relights her cigarette. She ain't thought about Billie in a long time. Years and years ago, in that picture of Billie they showed on the news, her black curly hair was pulled up tight into a high ponytail. She had on a pink shirt and pink striped shorts with white tube socks pulled above her ankles—that was the style then. She was drinking a glass of water, turned to the camera but looking up at someone else with big brown eyes. She was lost the news said, but even after she was found, Lola never saw her again.

BILLIE

HER FIRST NIGHT IN GREENDALE, SHE HAS A DREAM AND IN THIS
dream she is alone in a small spartan room: bare floorboards,
a single window. She is standing next to a gaunt man, pencil
gray, sitting at a table looking down at his watch, then out of
the window and up at the moon. The moon, in this dream, is
small and silver blue; it is glowing a hole in the sky. The man
keeps looking from his watch to the moon, saying: It's time.
Then the dream begins again and each time she feels sicker
because she knows that in a few minutes the world will end.

There is a large moth battering the bedroom window.
Rufus looks at her from where he lies on an old blanket.

"Bad dream," she tells him.

Rolling off of the partially deflated air mattress, she shuf-
fles into the closet-size bathroom, pulling on the light. The
sink almost juts over the toilet and there is barely room for
her knees when she sits.

Upon standing, she encounters a puckered reflection. Her cheek is creased and her eyes have shrunk. She rubs at the glass but it has gone dim as if the real mirror were waiting behind a fog.

In the bedroom, the orange-furred moth paces the screen. She unplugs the lamp, but the moth stays. There are no cars on the main road, no lights from distant shacks. "What does it want?" she asks Rufus.

He gets up, makes a circle, and lies back down. She nudges the gun sock closer to the bed with her foot, then lies down on her side so she can follow the moth's shuddering path over the dark glass. Maybe the moth is trying to tell her something, like birds sensing an oncoming storm.

She sits up, feeling for the lamp, and plugs it in. Rufus flicks an eye open, spots her, then shuts it again. She drags the mattress into the corner, taking a book from her suitcase, and props her pillows against the wall. From somewhere across the fields, dogs howl. Rufus barks under his breath, then groans.

"It's okay, boy," she says. "Hopefully."

When she had nightmares as a kid, she would go into her mother's room, kneel by the side of the bed, and whisper: "I'm thinking bad thoughts."

Her mother would roll to her without opening her eyes and say: "Think good ones."

And just like that her mother interrupted the end of the world.

IN THE MORNING, BILLIE DRESSES STANDING ON HER SUITCASE BE-cause the floor is fucking freezing. Not to mention the water heater is broken and she can't warm up with a hot shower. She fills the tiny bathroom sink with cold water and spot washes like a scullery maid.

In the living room, the sun is pouring through cracks in the front door. Her neck is aching. She fell asleep tipped over her book with her mouth open. Outside the sky is fairy-tale blue and the sun glosses the trees. She walks with Rufus through the woods and into the jubilant screech of birds.

Leaving the dog behind, she cruises antique stores that double as bail bond companies and ends up at a Walmart on the outskirts of town where she buys an AC unit, mini-fridge, coffeemaker, and space heater. At the register, there is a flock of white women in pink camo. The cashier leans over the credit card machine to tell her that hunting season is over except for spring turkey (three per season), frog (up to twenty-five per night), and it won't be squirrel until next month. In some godforsaken aisle, a toddler is shrieking.

Billie calls her uncle from the parking lot. They haven't spoken that much, and Jude thinks she should try and recon-nect. "So is there any family left in town? Like my cousins— Lola and Aleisha and Junior and everyone."

That last summer, a bandanna round her head to hold back her mane, the strawberries filling her shirt stained her stomach. They all tried to make juice by stomping on them in a big plastic bowl like somebody saw on *I Love Lucy*. Grandmomma Ruby, Daddy's momma, got mad at the mess so they went to live in the woods where they made slingshots and hunted squirrels and were trailed by bees.

"All those kids moved on with they own families." Her

uncle coughs. "You might not recall but their granddaddy was your great-uncle Floyd and he died a while back."

"Are you driving?"

"We can talk. Helps me stay awake."

In the parking spot in front of her, a mother with four kids gets out of a car from another era. The youngest three, near tears, all want to be picked up, the neon wax of whatever they've been eating burning around their mouths. The oldest one, already a little mother, picks up the baby and takes another by the hand.

"What about my father's old friends? Would any of them still be around?" His poet friends still call her sometimes from New York to get her to agree to a reprinting, even though she's not the literary executor, her uncle is.

"What, you writing a book?"

She smiles as the oldest kid catches her eye. "No, but I'm here so I might as well meet somebody."

"He was close to Sheila. But she passed a little while ago. She was cool, though she married herself a hardheaded motherfucker—excuse my language—Jerry Hopsen. Naw, most everybody who knew Cliff is dead or gone."

"Including you." She flips on the AC.

"I'm never far enough from Greendale."

"You only live an hour or two away. Why not move across the country, like to California or something?"

"Ain't that the million-dollar question. I been all over this country. I been to France two times. But I always come back to Mississippi."

"Why?"

"I don't know, but I always do."

SOMEWHERE BETWEEN MOBILE HOMES AND WRAPAROUND PORCHES, there is a neighborhood of modest cottages where the streets are named after trees. Billie pulls over in front of a row of mismatched furniture set out on the lawn of a burnt umber house, the only one on the block whose screen door and windows have bars and a little security sign stabbed in the grass by cement porch steps. A dark gray Cadillac is brooding under a low wooden carport built over the driveway with a sign nailed to its front: POSTED KEEP OUT. Looks like hardheaded Jerry Hopsen is having a garage sale.

A goateed man in his sixties who is probably Jerry is wheeling a trash can crammed with weeds to the curb. He stops and wipes his hands down the sides of his khaki shorts. "How you doing?"

Rufus jumps down from the backseat and Billie shuts the door. "Good, thanks." There is no shade on the street. The trees in the neighborhood are too thin, though his neatly trimmed grass is violently green.

"You looking for something in particular?"

"Not really. I just moved to town."

"Well, welcome to Greendale." He leaves the trash can and walks over. "Where you coming from?"

"Philadelphia."

"Mississippi?"

"No." She smiles. "The other one."

"What brings you here?"

She wanders over to a velour floral armchair. "I inherited a house. Well, the remains of one."

He checks the Victorian pedestal mailbox that matches his house, a Pony Express design on its front and HOPSEN glued on in black letters. "That there was my wife's. She passed last year."

Sheila's chair. "I'm sorry." Maybe her father sat in it. "How long have you lived in Greendale?"

He pulls out two letters and a grocery circular, thumbing through the mail. "All my days, child, all my days."

"Do you think you'll ever leave?"

"Nope. So whose mansion you inherit?"

"I think you know him: Clifton James?"

Hopsen looks up. "Cliff James? We were in school together."

"I know. I'm his daughter, Billie."

"Isn't that something," he says, walking up to her. "I see him in the eyes. But now you know who you look like is your mother."

They shake hands. He is standing too close. Not so close that they might touch but so she can't comfortably look into his face.

"I met your mother a time or two when she come out here. But she ain't ever stay long. You know how it was. People weren't comfortable about the races mixing. Some folks still ain't."

Her parents were married in Pennsylvania because in early 1967 their interracial marriage was a felony in Mississippi. It is hard for her to imagine their marriage being a crime, but sometimes it is hard to imagine having ever had parents.

"Cliff James." He shakes his head. "I remember the day he won the school spelling bee. We was in fifth grade. He was real smart but that day he was just plain lucky. They were giving him words like *oblong* and *lemon* and he got himself a trophy big as he was." He scratches his goatee. "I was real surprised that he came back. Because man, all I could remember was how when we was young he couldn't wait to get out."

"Maybe he missed it here."

"I did say to him, I said Cliff, you should've stayed out east. And if he had, who knows. Might still be alive."

There are mismatched glasses set out on one of the tables. She picks up a purple BLESSED mug. Of course, there are so many ways it might not have happened.

"Well," says Hopsen, "ain't nobody know what might have been but God. Hey there, dog." He holds out a hand. Rufus sniffs then licks, thinks about jumping.

"Rufus, sit." She snaps her fingers.

"Your mama come with you?"

Rufus licks her knee. "She died."

Hopsen nods magisterially, as if the death of their women squares them in his mind. "I am sorry to hear that." He folds his mail under his arm. "You plan on staying here in Greendale for good?"

"No, just another week or so. You wouldn't know anything about the other tenant houses, would you? I thought there used to be others out there."

"They ain't none where you are no more. Those are all gone. Including the house my wife grew up in. Old John McGee, the father of the one who's alive now, sold most of that land to an agricultural company."

"So who would you say is my closest neighbor?"

"The McGees."

She wipes off her knee. "Your wife was close to my father?"

"Who told you that?"

"My uncle."

"Don't know what Dee would know. He was nothing but a kid back then. We all grew up together. Me, Sheila, and Cliff. Sheila's family lived next to his."

"Do you remember the last time you saw my daddy?"

He shakes his head. "It was a long time ago. When you get old you realize that you never know that the last time is the last." He looks at the table. "You see anything you like? I'll give you half off."

"Sheila's chair." She takes out her wallet. "And this mug." She follows him over to a metal strongbox where he counts out her change.

"Your car ain't big enough for this chair."

"Can you hold on to it until my uncle comes?"

"Dee drives a truck, but he don't own one. Tell you what, I'll get my son to come by and drop it off tonight. He ain't doing nothing."

"Thanks. That's really generous of you." She wraps the end of Rufus's leash around her wrist, her fingers feeling to where it has frayed. "This might sound a little strange . . ."

Hopsen looks at her as if he knows what she might say.

"But did you know me?"

There is a movement at one of the windows behind him, something bumping against the blinds, making them shudder in the heat.

"You remember what all happened back then?"

One summer night in 1972, when she was four years old,

her father was walking in the woods when he fell and hit his head. He died while she was asleep in the house.

"Not really," she says.

"Baby, that's one of them things, either you do, or you don't." Hopsen picks a candy wrapper off the grass and walks back to the trash can, lifting up the lid and throwing it in. "I only know you from that picture of you that come on the news."

"What do you mean on the news?"

"When you was missing."

A white heat rolls up her back. "I don't know what you're talking about."

He stares at her. "They couldn't find you when they found your daddy, so they put a picture of you up on the news. Ain't nobody tell you?"

"No, no one." It's hard to breathe because of her heartbeat. "Are you sure that was me?"

He knocks a few blades of grass from his pants. "That's what I recall. But all that matters is they found you, didn't they."

HOPSEN

AFTER ALL THIS TIME, HE CAN'T HARDLY BELIEVE IT, CLIFF'S CHILD
come back. Coming all the way down here and for what?
Nothing for her here but an old shack that ain't worth the
saving with the roof likely rotted and the insulation too.
He wasn't expecting Billie James to show up like that. All
grown, asking questions. He closes the front door behind
him, the dark of the house a relief.

He sits down on the couch in front of the TV, a red
headline smearing along the bottom of the screen. Can't
read it without his glasses. He turns it up. It's too quiet now
without Sheila. Though there are times in the morning when
he swears he hears her slippers across the floor. But those
old beat-up slippers are still in her closet, waiting for her to
put her little painted toes in them. His daughter wants to
go through it all. Just tell me the day, she reminds him at
least twenty-five times a week. But Sheila's clothes are too

nice to give away or junk to anybody but him. It was his daughter's idea to have the garage sale, though he hasn't told her yet that none of her mother's clothes are out. He goes to the kitchen and wipes down the sink, rubbing at the grime around the tap, and starts the dishwasher. He's been a neat freak ever since the army.

He leans over the clean sink and lathers his hands, running them under warm water. His son and daughter do come over and visit. His son too much. Boy don't like to work, says he's discriminated against because of his record. But what's keeping him from borrowing the lawn mower and knocking on doors and getting some money in his pocket? It's a struggle to understand where his head is at. The boy can't stick to one woman neither. He is a good-looking boy. His mother prayed on it. But the way he sees it, the only thing God has granted the boy is the sense not to have kids. At least there is that. But he drinks too much at the club, like his grandfather did, and the funny thing is that his son thinks he don't know nothing about it.

He turns the water off. Maybe it's time to get himself a dog. When Sheila was alive they appreciated having the freedom to travel. She loved cruises, especially that one they took to Jamaica. He always said he wanted to take one of them Alaskan ones and she would look at him funny. The woman hated to be cold. It's real strange, even if it don't make no sense, to think of her now in the cold cold ground. His baby, his little Scoop. A name from their youth when he could scoop her whole body up in his arms and go running off down the road.

He walks back into the living room and peeks out the

window into the front yard. Got to make sure nobody goes off running with the garage sale. The child is still out there. What's she waiting on? He ain't wanna get mixed up in it all. He lets go of the curtain and sits. He has always made sure that he's been around for his son. Basketball games, school concerts, and all that mess. How many hours of slow-as-molasses baseball games has he sat through? Never his sport. His own father died on the chain gang. A heart attack or sunstroke, he'll never know because the prison never cared to figure out. It was enough that he was dead and couldn't work no more. If his son would just keep himself busy, get a job, he wouldn't drink. But he's too damn pigheaded to know what's good for him. He turns off the TV, puts on his glasses, and picks up the crossword he started in the morning's paper.

Sheila wanted to send the boy away, get him out of Mississippi, send him to her family in Chicago. But they got their own nonsense going on up there. He didn't want his son involved with no gangs. At least down here the boy's around the fools he grew up with, the ones his father knows. One of them boys is bound to make something of themselves one day and influence him right. Now a real man, a real man can make something out of nothing. A black man in this world knows the battle's uphill. The last czar of Russia, eight letters down. Didn't he watch something at the hospital about the Russian Revolution? Might be Alexander but that would be nine.

Sheila thought he pushed Marcus too hard, but anybody can see it's the opposite. Maybe he's wrong, maybe it would be better if the boy had a family, someone to provide for.

He gets up and goes to the window, moving the curtain. Billie James is still standing with her dog at the bottom of the yard. He'll go back out to the sale when she leaves. It's not that he can't talk to her, of course he can. He just did. He shouldn't have said what he said about her missing. But it seems like she turned out fine. Don't seem disturbed or nothing, not sick in the head. Does sound kinda white though. He didn't know that she lost her mother. Now that's a shame cause a girl needs her mother. No consolation for a loss like that.

Maybe he needs a little part-time job now that he's retired. It's too easy to end up walking from room to room all day like he crazy. All night for that matter. But it tires him out to talk to folks these days. It's not that he don't want to talk, but that he only wants to talk to Scoop.

He lets go of the curtain in case Billie looks back, wiping his damp hands down the front of his pants, and goes into the kitchen and opens the fridge. It's not too early for a beer, almost noon. Saturday anyway. He didn't mean to tell Billie all that, going on like an old man. Thought she already knew. Real strange they ain't told her. But then it seemed like she didn't remember nothing, which is the best thing for everybody.

If Sheila was here she would have invited the girl in, asked her to dinner. But he can hardly do that when he'll be heating up some frozen mess in the microwave unless his daughter happens to come over and cook. He opens the beer and goes back to the living room window. Billie has started to walk down the street. He puts the beer on a coaster. It's sad that the girl ain't have either of her parents. Though what happened to Cliff he brought on his own damn self. He had nothing to do with it. He drinks, going back to the cross-word on the coffee table, then puts the beer down and goes to the door to offer the girl the use of his lawn mower.

BILLIE

HOPSEN'S NEIGHBORHOOD IS MAINLY SMALL COTTAGES AND churches. Some neatly done up in American flags and shrubs, others bald and paint sore, windows badly patched with plywood. Down a dead-end street, there is a house with a homemade neon cross showcased in the front yard. The cross is taller than she is and the bulbs lining the wooden frame around the cross remind her of an open casket. Rufus won't go near the house and she has to drag him to the chain-link fence to get a better look. The house still has its Christmas decorations up. A red and green wreath shriveled against the front door. HAPPY BIRTHDAY, JESUS. FOREVER.

Billie calls Jude, but Jude knows nothing about it. Her mother never said anything about Billie having gone missing. But then her mother was selective with the stories she told. Hers were stories of extremes: cults and forgotten mystics, medieval heretics, abducted princelings. Billie phones her uncle but it goes straight to voice mail. At least she's seeing him soon. Jerry Hopsen must be confused, mixing her up with someone else—it was thirty years ago. Missing missing missing. Where does that live in her body?

"What kind of dog is that?" A young boy with a hint of a lisp is coming down his driveway holding a pit bull on a too-thin leash.

"A Lab mix." She steers Rufus off the road and onto a lawn, since there are no sidewalks.

"He a male or female?" The boy uses both hands to restrain his dog but his eyes are on her; his face eager, sweet. "Mine's name is Red Boy."

"Good name. This is Rufus."

The dogs sniff each other until she starts walking again. The boy follows her as if he belongs to her. She can't tell if he's friendly or lonely. He won't pet Rufus, too worried he'll bite. Instead, he dances around whenever Rufus pants near. Together, they pass a small brick church with marble-size holes in its screens and milky blue stained glass across the tops of its windows.

"Listen," says the boy, stopping.

Coming from the window is the swell and call of a Baptist choir. Something unbuckles in her chest. "Pretty," she says.

"Do you live here?" He bends to scratch his dog's neck.

"For a little while."

The boy looks up at her. "Maybe we can walk our dogs together every day."

"Maybe." She smiles.

"My church is downtown. Where do you go to church?"

"I don't."

"Are you saved?" Above his head, a cloud of gnats desperately orbit one another in the sun.

She leans forward to look through a big tear in one of the screens. Not many in the pews. A few paper fans waving, the pastor leaning back in his robe and red chair, behind him a dark brown Jesus on the wall. That face. She looks back at the boy. That face. A man's voice pressed tight to a microphone lets the agony of the faithful out.

"I guess not," she says.

BACK IN THE CAR, BILLIE DRIVES THROUGH THE NEON GLARE OF GAS stations and fast-food chains and convicts in their orange vests cleaning the side of the road, past flea markets as quiet as the grave and trailers on stilts alternating with shacks sunk into the ground. She drives until there are only fields and homes that look so abandoned she can't tell if anyone lives there, even with broken lawn mowers in the yard, or watered armchairs sagging on the porch, or the occasional kid's bike lying on its side in the gravel like the skeleton of a candy-colored insect. Only the tiny white clapboard churches look recently inhabited, like someone has just finished arranging the slightly crooked black letters of the signs that advise her to TELL JESUS ABOUT IT, or warn DEATH IS COMING ARE YOU PREPARED? Today she feels like these places look, like she has been scattered in the rain, never to be picked up again.

Back at the house, she stocks the warped plywood cupboard above the kitchen counter with substandard groceries: plastic cheese and counterfeit jambalaya. She's taken a detour into somebody else's small town life of revival meetings and off-brand soda.

After hosing the cobwebs off of what screens the house has left, she finally takes a shower, since the plumber has been by to install a new water heater. Good thing she got that money from Gran. She turbans her hair in a towel and turns on the water. The harsh spray of the cheap showerhead plugs her ears. She steps in and closes her eyes, turning her aching shoulders to the hot water. Okay, think. She would be on her cot in the dark with the box fan churning. The night dark, sticky, gigantic. The door creaks, someone coming in. They pick her up and carry her out of the house. Did she know them and trust them or was it a stranger? How did they get to the next place? Drive? Walk? In her pajamas? This could be it as much as anything else she might imagine. She twists the hot-water knob. Okay, maybe think less about the event but of the feeling. Lonely. That feels true. But is that just what she expects she would feel? A little kid taken away from her daddy, a little kid whose daddy is taken away? This is useless. She turns off the shower.

As she steps out, a mouse darts out from behind the toilet. "Shit!" There's a crack in the wall. She crouches down and, seeing no rodent paws, stuffs the hole with toilet paper. Might not do much since it's only one-ply.

She unwinds the towel from her head and dries her body. "Shit." She forgot to use soap.

Outside, dragonflies flicker above the yard. Rufus chews the grass until he finds a half-eaten lizard and chews on that. The house needs some kind of landscaping at the front, shrubs or hedges. She walks to the side of the porch and peers into the woods between the house and creek. Maybe somebody didn't take her. Maybe that night she woke up and went looking for her father. Maybe she got lost or scared and hid, or had a *mésaventure* as her mother would say, an accident in Old French.

Headlights come up the dirt road, gravel stinging the wheels of a truck distinct against the flat fields of no crops. Billie waves. Rufus runs down the drive, barking. The truck rattles up to the porch and Mr. Hopsen and his son get out. She walks with them to the back of the truck where a lawn mower and a dead woman's armchair sit.

MILES SOUTH OF THE WIDE BLOCKS THAT ARE GREENDALE'S HISTORIC downtown of Greek Revival law firms, of vacant buildings with old Coca-Cola ads tattooed to their sides, of ancient, craggy men on bicycles wearing shrunken baseball caps, is her uncle's apartment in what used to be a motel.

It's hot. A hint of the vacuum-sealed wet of a Mississippi summer in the air. She turns off the AC and rolls the windows down, letting in a warm wash of heat, then shakes the last of the potato chips into her mouth. What the hell. Where is her uncle? She's been in this parking lot for an hour and he hasn't returned any of her calls. They were supposed to meet here an hour ago.

Now it's nine o'clock and the roads are overrun by boys in big-wheeled Cadillacs. C'mon, motherfucker, they whoop over a serrated beat. Friday night and the young gleam in the gas stations and drive-thrus of this tiny city where the level of poverty (she's read) is almost 40 percent.

Billie gets out and tours the parking lot. Each tenant has distinguished their room by the way that they cover the long window beside their front door. Some are sealed tight with tinfoil, others with a printed sheet, but her uncle's window on the second floor is bare. A few people are sitting outside of their doors on plastic chairs. Nothing moves except for a can or cigarette. The light from passing cars gives their faces the sheen of old master paintings. Hendrick ter Brugghen's *Melancholia*. The contemplation and the shadows. Nothing is happening but a wanting something to happen.

A white woman wearing a long T-shirt covering her shorts is standing on the corner like she's waiting for a bus, but there's no bus stop sign. It doesn't look like she's been able to shower for the last week, and her expression says her ride is never going to come. She paces, the flip-flops askew on her bitterly dry feet.

Jude calls, but Billie doesn't answer. She needs to be vigilant. She gets back in the car. She needs to let Rufus out soon and it's almost a two-hour drive back. Maybe wait fifteen more minutes. She slides deeper into the driver's seat, exhausted from mowing the yard, which she's never done before, having never had a yard. A mosquito bounces off the windshield and sinks into the dark interior of the car. Then through the bug-smeared glass, an older black man followed by a white woman goes up the steps and toward her uncle's apartment.

She hops out, slamming the car door and hurrying after them. "Uncle Dee?" she calls from the bottom of the stairs.

Her father's little brother turns, a straw cowboy hat curling on his head. Above the white V-neck under his Hawaiian shirt, a scar over his collarbone moves, knotted and dark.

"It's Billie!" she shouts, taking the steps two at a time.

The blond woman stays by the door, impatient to get

inside, but her uncle meets her halfway down the balcony, hugging her and leaving a film of beer and Old Spice. He holds her out from him. "Lord, you look just the same as when you was a kid. Sorry I'm so late. I tend to get my days and nights mixed up on the road."

"It's okay." She forgives him instantly.

"Man"—her uncle shakes his head—"I can't believe how long it's been." He walks her to the apartment and the blond woman moves back as he unlocks the door. "Last time I seen you, I was a teenager babysitting you."

Her uncle is close on fifty and missing two teeth, one on the bottom and one on the top. The blond woman looks at least fifteen years younger. But it is hard to read the old acne scars, thin platinum hair, spike-thick mascara, fake designer purse, and the crooked music note tattoo below her mini-skirt and above her knee.

As they go in, Billie turns to her. "I'm Dee's niece, Billie."

"He told me. Lacey." The woman walks in front of her.

"It ain't much," says her uncle, turning on a lamp, which illuminates an office chair, a cracked brown couch, and a tilt-ing carpeted floor the color of grease. The room is crammed with furniture from a life he must have lived a few lives ago. On the phone, he called his place a step above prison. She thought he was being funny.

"I haven't been home long enough to clean it up."

"It's nice," she says, the lie too soft to be heard.

Billie sits on the couch by the front window while her uncle goes over to the kitchenette, waving away a few fruit flies and filling a glass of water from the tap. "Thirsty?" he asks. Billie shakes her head, but Lacey sits in an ancient wicker chair in the corner and puts out her hand. He sets Lacey a glass by a dead plant on top of the AC unit, then takes a tall boy from the minifridge.

"I can't stand this humidity already. It's different in Nebraska." Her uncle takes off his Hawaiian shirt and throws it at the bed, not picking it up when it flutters to the floor. "This whole damn part of town is all concrete."

"I guess the cold snap's over," Billie says. From where she is sitting, the air from the AC unit is wet and rubbery.

"Nebraska? When were you in Nebraska?" asks Lacey.

"Last year." Uncle Dee wheels himself on the office chair to the middle of the room and opens his beer. "Back when I was full-time. Now I work on an as-needed basis. Any more trouble out there at the house?"

"No. I think I just got spooked," Billie says, tracing the blister forming on her hand where she held the lawn mower too tight. "I did hear some wind chimes. Guess that would be coming from the McGees."

"Naw, they too far off."

"Well, I doubt a thief is stalking me holding wind chimes."

"We got all kind of characters out in the Delta," he says.

"What do you think about me renting out the house? I'd fix it up a little more of course."

"Don't care what you do with it." He cocks his head back to drink, almost closing his eyes.

He's been like this about the house since she first called him after Gran died. She wanted to see if he wanted to live there. He didn't.

"I met Jerry Hopsen on Saturday."

He opens his eyes. "How did that happen?"

"You said his wife, Sheila, was close to Daddy so I looked him up."

He stares at her. "And what did that old so-and-so have to say about my brother?"

Her eyes flicker to Lacey, who is examining her cuticles in the wicker chair. "He said they all grew up together—him and Sheila and Daddy."

"That it?"

"That and he didn't know me."

"What in the hell he mean by that?"

"That he never met me before. Is that true?"

"Might could be. Last time you were here was a long time ago, baby. I was still in high school." Her uncle leans back in his chair. "Cliff didn't like people who weren't family coming over when you was in town. If he wanted to see folks he would go to Avalon."

"Wait, Avalon? That's a real place?"

"Old juke joint we used to go to off 61."

"Just like in his poem."

"Oh yeah, I remember that one."

"Is it still open? Can we go there?"

He laughs. "Baby, it's been closed down for years. Folks ain't into jukes no more. They go to the club. You want to go to Avalon?"

"Yes. Absolutely."

"I'll take you this weekend. Be here at noon on Sunday. Sheila . . ." Her uncle shakes his head then grins. "Man, you never forget brown sugar sweet as that."

Lacey swipes at him halfheartedly and collapses over her

own thighs, suddenly seeming drunk, though Billie hasn't noticed her drinking anything except water.

"What you do for work again?" he says.

"I'm a grant writer. It's for a good nonprofit, but pretty boring, though I do get to work mostly from home."

Her uncle is looking down into his beer as if he is trying to see something written on the bottom of the can. "I'd like to sit home doing my work."

The chemical wail of a car alarm comes from the parking lot. Lacey doesn't sit up, her forehead poured onto mottled knees.

Her uncle sets his sweating tall boy between his feet. "Be careful in them woods with all the snakes."

"Wouldn't my dog scare them off?"

"More like to get bit. The Delta can be rough on a dog."

She glances over at the fallen Lacey. "Seems she's no longer with us." She looks at her uncle. "You know, when I saw Mr. Hopsen he told me something I've never heard before. It's really crazy. He said that the night Daddy died, I went missing, and that my picture was on the news. Is that true?"

Her uncle shakes his head. "Why he tell you that? He's representing it all wrong. Of course that fool would. He don't know nothing about it."

"Was I on the news?"

His dark eyes meet hers. "Your momma didn't tell you nothing about it?"

"Not a thing."

"It's all right, honey, it ain't that big a deal. The police were so dumb they couldn't find you sleeping in some blankets in the closet. So they made you a missing person because you were so little and we all lost our minds."

"The closet? Why was I there?"

"I don't know. That's where he kept your toys. Maybe you got scared. But they got Momma so riled up she had everybody looking for you and somebody sent your picture to the local news. Then a couple hours later, there you were."

"I can't believe my mom didn't tell me about it."

"Some times are so bad people can't ever talk about it."

Billie is still for a moment. "I better get going. It'll take me a while to get back and I need to let out the dog." She feels for the keys in her purse and is stabbed by an uncapped pen.

Her uncle walks her to the door and follows her out onto the balcony. They both lean on the railing, looking into the parking lot.

"It's really good to see you," she says.

"Good to see you too. Good to reconnect." He coughs, then turns to light a cigarette, cupping the flame. "Don't bother asking Jerry nothing."

The cars below wash in, rushing up to the stoplight only to brake, red above red.

"I'm not planning on it."

He nods. "Good, good. I ain't trying to tell you what to do."

Her uncle is singing something that she can't make out over the rattle of window units. He coughs again. He's still handsome but too thin. He was Grandmomma Ruby's miracle baby, born after she was forty. Because she'd never gotten pregnant after Daddy, Mom said she thought the doctors had given her one of those "Mississippi appendectomies," or forced sterilizations.

"Do you want me to get you some water?" she asks.

He holds up his hand, steadying himself with the other on the railing. "Naw, I'm just coming down with a cold. Always do this time of year. My summer cold."

THAT LAST SUMMER WITH HER MOTHER WAS SO HOT THAT THEY GAVE up cooking and ate everything raw, cold, ready made. Popsicles, red grapes, hard cheese. They gave up on surgery/radiation/chemotherapy, gave up on her being cured, and visitors came to witness Mom's fading mortality, avoiding talking about her ruthless diarrhea or needle-bruised hands.

At the end of that summer, Billie was nineteen and just starting her second year at Temple University. She rarely slept at the dorm, barely knew her roommate, a redhead from Yardley who slept on the bottom bunk and played the violin. When she came home after class, instead of doing homework she read Weldon Kees, who'd had a dog named Lonesome and parked his Plymouth on the side of the Golden Gate Bridge then disappeared. That summer she had decided that her father might not be dead. After all, she had never been to the so-called funeral and seen the "body." Maybe he was like the pugilist-poet Arthur Cravan, a nephew of Oscar Wilde and husband of Mina Loy, who disappeared sailing along the coast of Mexico, but might have actually died an old amnesiac in Chile. Then she wondered if maybe her father had killed himself and searched in the library through African American anthologies for poets who had committed suicide and found only one: Mae Virginia Cowdery, 1909–1953.

Her mother spent those days getting smaller under a blanket on the couch facing the balcony. They lived near a mosque and she liked to hear the call to prayer. Billie liked to lie on top of the blanket, near her mother's hip, but not on her waist because of the fluid. Her mother could lie for hours, her head wrapped in a scarf, watching the light enter and retreat.

The last week before she moved into hospice, she told Billie: "You're going to need to be tough."

"I know." Billie had actually been thinking about turning tough—how she was going to start carrying a knife and wear all black and be alone like a monk, a spiritual athlete who contemplated nature and didn't give a shit about what other people said.

"You have to be tough."

"You said." Jude told her to accept whatever her mother threw at her and gave her Thich Nhat Hanh's *The Miracle of Mindfulness* and Ram Dass's *Be Here Now,* which Billie accidentally left on the train.

"You'll never be white enough or black enough for some people."

Billie sat up. Her mother had never said that.

"I know. But what can I say?" Her mother pushed up her sleeves, the veins in her arms red and swollen with collapse. "We didn't want it to be a burden. We wanted it to be beautiful, and it was."

Then they both were silent hearing the muezzin's labyrinthine tenor from across the street. Billie didn't really believe that her mother could go and leave her here. She knew she would sink into the earth the moment her mother did.

"Well"—her mother shifted under the blanket to reach her glass of lemon water—"at least I get to die high in bed."

Her mother was a medievalist specializing in the Black Death, Chaucer, the Jacquerie, the pillaging free companies, the Hundred Years' War—even small talk with her could be morbid.

"I thought we would be pulled over one night on a dark and empty road and made to get out of the car just like in the other Philadelphia." Her mother would return to this until she stopped speaking. "It was war in Mississippi."

"It's all right now, Mom."

"I'm so glad you were asleep," her mother said, looking out at the balcony. "But where did you go after that?"

"It's okay. I'm here." Billie stroked her mother's hand.

Was that it? Had Mom been trying to tell her that she had gone missing?

LOLA

IT'S NOT LIKE SHE DIDN'T LISTEN. SHE LISTENED AND THEN MADE HER decision. The right damn decision far as she's concerned.

It's a little sad to pass these big houses down the main boulevard with their white columns and gilt lanterns and long semicircle driveways under beautiful oak trees, their branches draped above them like these houses are protected, special. Inside, the air condition has probably chilled the glass of the windows and the tiles of the foyer where an entryway table holds a big vase of fresh orchids or maybe peonies (they're both in season). Don't nobody else think it's strange how close these houses are to her nana's house where damn near everything is falling in on itself like it's in a twenty-four-hour earthquake? At night, they ain't even have streetlights to see where they going, like they still living in the days before electricity.

Lola drives over the bridge into the acres of open fields.

It looks like most of the cotton seed has been planted. She never chopped cotton herself. But her mother did as soon as she was too big to ride on the end of the cotton sack while Nana dragged it up and down the turnrows. For a while, Nana worked in the fields and at the white lady's house. But then she took in some washing and the only land she worked was her own vegetable garden.

Lola pulls up next to the house. There's no car but she can hear a dog barking inside. After Cousin Cliff died, Momma would sometimes drive by here on the way to her auntie's house, saying they were lucky to not wake up one morning and find out *they* didn't have a daddy. Her brother rolled his eyes and slouched back, pulling up the hood of his Chicago Bears sweatshirt. When it first happened, he told Lola that Billie had found Cousin Cliff's body and the shock of it killed her. Lola didn't believe him. Aleisha had told her a much better story where Cousin Cliff died in Billie's arms and she carried him all the way up to the house. Junior said that Billie ran away and was living on a raft on the Tallahatchie, and all summer they looked for her with the toy compass out of a box of Cracker Jack. It was the least they could do, Billie being the youngest.

Momma should have been saying imagine waking up one morning and you *have* a daddy. Which is kind of what's happening, now that he's trying to be more in Lola's life. They talk on the phone every other week. He calls, not her. He asks about work. Tells her he loves her. But how is that possible when he doesn't even know who she is?

Nana says he was never good with children. Then maybe he shouldn't have had any. The strange thing is that sometimes Lola defends him to her brother. Her brother won't talk to him out of respect for their mother. It ain't right, her brother says. But it's not about who is right, it's about wanting to understand who her father is.

The men in her life seem like they're around just to disrupt her peace. The other night, she was at her boyfriend's apartment, rinsing a glass at the kitchen sink, when his phone kept ringing on the counter. It must've rung three different times. He was in the bathroom. She leaned over and saw the name of a woman he'd never mentioned. She didn't say a word about it, but when he came out of the bathroom it was like he knew something was up and started talking about them taking a trip next month to the Bahamas. Lola lied and said she had to travel for work.

She gets out of the car and walks around the house. Cousin Cliff's house is smaller than she remembers. How the hell did all the cousins fit in there? Sitting on the couch with Popsicles watching *Scooby-Doo,* or *Underdog,* or the *Jackson 5ive* cartoon. Taking turns wearing the platform shoes one of Cousin Cliff's girlfriends had left lying around. And why would Billie want to stay in this creepy old shack? You ain't catch her sleeping in the house where her father had died. Lola gets back in the car and sits in the driver's seat with the door open, taking a magazine from her purse. This ain't the way she was expecting to spend her Saturday, but she has to drive back up to Memphis tomorrow. At least this month's issue of *Essence* is on Natalie Cole and Nona Gaye, and apparently Maya Angelou is gonna tell her how to love herself at every age. Just as she's reading that Marvin Gaye's daughter had a three-year relationship with Prince (she forgot about that!) a car turns off the main road and onto the gravel drive, parking behind her.

The woman in the driver's seat pushes up her black sunglasses until they touch a big bun of curls piled on top of her head. She still looks like the little girl in the picture above Nana's TV of all the cousins living and dead, before they left the Delta or rocked a uniform with MDOC CONVICT stamped on the back, before they never called or still lived with their momma, before they had five kids or lived alone in a two-bedroom condo in Northern Virginia.

Billie gets out of the car, not smiling like she was in the picture, like they all were (except for Aleisha) because they ain't know yet. They still thought that they would be rich when they grew up and buy their momma a big house, and that the Lord's love would save them from a world that might find them too dangerous to live.

"Lola?" Billie walks toward her. "I can't— You look the same." They hug in front of the porch steps.

"I know maybe you didn't want us disturbing you, but I'm no good at listening."

"You're not disturbing me. I thought you all had moved away."

"Well, I do live in Memphis." Lola pulls back so she can see her. "So let me ask you a question, am I intruding? Dee said you needed your space."

"What? No, I never said anything like that."

"See, now that's what I thought. It's probably what he thinks you need. You know how he is."

"I don't know why he said that. Want to come in? Let me

grab the dog first. He's friendly, but it takes him a minute to calm down. You aren't allergic or scared of dogs, are you?"

"It's all good. Bring on the pack."

Billie goes into the house and comes out holding the dog by its collar. He licks Lola's jeans and nuzzles her hand.

"His name is Rufus."

Lola pets his head. "Hi there, Rufus."

"I inherited him from my grandmother."

Lola follows Billie and the dog into the house. She never thought she'd be walking in here again. Billie offers her the only chair in the room and drags a foldout chair in from the porch.

"So I have coffee, whiskey, and tap water. What will it be?"

"I can tell you that I don't want water."

Billie laughs and goes into the kitchen, coming back with two paper cups of whiskey. "Let's toast."

Lola raises her cup. "To 'Rockin' Robin.'"

"Oh my god, you remember that?"

Their paper cups smash together, almost collapsing.

"Girl, I remember all the singing contests. I'm still proud I won with 'Clean Up Woman.'"

"Wait, who sang that again?"

"Ms. Betty Wright."

"Man, it's weird to be back here."

"And here you are by the grace of God." Lola raises her whiskey. They toast again and drink. "This is good."

"I don't do cheap whiskey."

"Mind if I take a tour?"

"Go ahead. I'll see you in thirty-five seconds."

Lola walks through the house. In the bedroom, a suit-case and a stack of books sit in the middle of the floor. A damp towel hangs over the closet's doorknob. The kitchen is decrepit, but the living room has been blessed by a calendar of Dr. King and the Kennedys hanging above Billie's head as she sits curled up in the folding chair.

"All right, girl, why you staying here and not a motel?"

"It's not that bad." Billie straightens her legs. "And it's mine. Rufus!"

Lola picks up her cup before the dog drinks it. "I would've thought this place would have a leaking roof, mice, and who knows what else."

"Well, there is a mouse living in the bathroom. But he's very polite."

"Oh Lord. You know I was in Philly for a conference once." And they could have passed each other on the street. "How much longer you staying here?"

Billie takes her hair out of the bun. She looks a little like Marvin Gaye's second wife, Nona Gaye's momma. The one who was only seventeen when they met. It must be the freckles.

"Less than a week now. This is my vacation. How's Alei-sha?"

"Poor Aleisha, nobody ever told her she could be some-body. She got four too many kids."

"How many does she have total?"

"Four."

Billie laughs. "That's so you. Does she live around here?"

"She moved down to Hattiesburg."

"I'd like to give her a call. You know, I almost came back

here after my mother died." She rubs her eye, smudging mascara underneath. "I was going to drive across the country, maybe fall off the edge when I got to the Pacific."

"I'm sorry about your mother."

Billie stands. "Thanks. Let's sit on the porch—is that okay?"

They go out and sit side by side on the top step. They've sat here before, but last time they had Silly Putty.

Lola wipes the lipstick from the edge of her cup. "How come you didn't come to his funeral?"

"My mom said I was too little." Billie finishes her whiskey and crushes the paper cup in her hand. "She never wanted to come back." Across the road, a line of birds rise and fall in the field. "It made sense to me. She was here during the Movement and then my father died here."

"The Movement broke a lot of people." Lola pushes a splinter of wood back into the step. "Do you remember him?"

"A little bit. She talked about him. Got me his books. Showed me pictures. But I have different questions now."

"You could talk to Dee."

Billie snorts. "I try. He's not very forthcoming. How's Junior?"

"He's doing good, emotionally. He was in prison for a while. Got mixed up with the wrong people, wanted to be living that type of lifestyle until he finally figured out it's all an illusion. Nana sent him down to one of our cousins who lives in Tampa." Lola finishes her whiskey.

Billie stretches her legs down the steps, letting her head drop to her chest. "What was he in for?" She sits up.

"Drugs." A line of sweat slides down Lola's back, but the

heat relaxes her, the way it asks her to give in. "You know, when you left, we wondered where you had gone. For all we knew, you'd been abducted by aliens."

"So I was definitely missing? How long?"

"I don't remember. I was only seven at the time. Nobody told you?"

Billie looks at her. "That's weird, isn't it?"

"Maybe your mom didn't want to traumatize you, or maybe she didn't want to retraumatize herself."

Billie turns toward the side of the porch. "When I was little, I was scared of these woods at night. I don't think I would've gone out there looking for him. Unless he called me, or it sounded like he was in trouble, maybe then I would have. And you know what else I don't think I would have done? Hidden in the closet, which is what Uncle Dee said I did. Because I was scared of the closet too."

"Dee said you were in the closet the whole time? That don't sound right."

"Yeah, apparently I fell asleep in there and they couldn't find me. He said it was for a couple hours, or a few hours, which doesn't really seem long enough for it to go up on the news. Do you remember if it was the morning news?"

"I don't know. It was daytime."

The dog leaps up on the porch and Billie scratches his neck. "Shit. I think there's something on him."

Lola leans over and looks through his fur. "Tick."

"What?" Billie lifts her hands. "I just gave him a disgusting tick-and-flea treatment before we got here."

"This is the Delta. You can't beat our version of nature." Lola gets a pair of tweezers out of her purse.

"Poor dog." Billie pets his nose.

"I'll show you how to do it, but you better check him when he comes in or the ticks'll get on you. You got rubbing alcohol?"

"All I have is ibuprofen."

"You better get some so you can clean it later." Lola kneels on the top step. "So look, you get as close to the skin as you can." Lola brings the tweezers around the tick's body.

"Gross." Billie looks away.

"Girl, pay attention. Then you pull up, but don't squeeze because you don't want to leave the head in." Lola pulls it out then walks inside, calling back, "Then flush it down the toilet."

"Can you grab the whiskey from the fridge?"

When she comes back with the bottle, Billie is stroking the dog's forehead. "Your first tick, buddy." Billie holds out an uncrumpled cup. "A double, please."

"You squeamish." Lola takes off the top and pours them both some whiskey.

"I'm fine with my blood just not other creatures'." Billie gets up and herds the dog back into the house. She comes back and sits on the bottom step. "So can I tell you about something strange?"

Lola sips this whiskey slowly. After all, she still has to drive back to Nana's. "Please do."

"I haven't told anyone, but I think you'll understand. So the night I got here, I went out for a walk by the creek and when I came back all of the lights were off, and I am pretty sure that I left at least one on. But when I went into the house, there was no one there."

"Nothing was taken?"

"Nope." Billie picks up a twig and traces a circle in the dirt.

"Then either somebody's trying to scare you or wants you to save on your electricity bill." Lola takes her phone out of her purse. No service. "You're definitely not gonna be living here full-time, right? You don't want to be hanging around with folks still mad they lost the Civil War."

Billie almost spits out her whiskey. "Oh my god."

"Girl, I'm serious."

"It's 2003. That's just like a few morbidly disturbed old people."

"Maybe they don't know it's the Civil War they still mad about."

"You mean the War of Northern Aggression?"

"You laughing, but nowadays, folks think they ain't racist cause they got a black friend at work. But we ain't friends when I've never sat down to a dinner you made me at your house. No girl, we just need all that hateful trash gone and then Mississippi would be all right, black folks could finally heal."

"Don't you think a lot of people need to heal?"

Lola purses her lips. "It's like this: white people have invented their fears about us and tried their damn best to make them true, but our fears about white people have always been real. White people have always had conspiracy theories about black people, because you can't trust the people you're trying to hold down. You know there used to be this one conspiracy theory that Abraham Lincoln was Jefferson Davis's illegitimate half brother?"

"I don't get it. What would that prove?"

"That the war really wasn't about slavery, that it was some kinda family feud."

Billie tosses the stick into the grass. "You know how it is around here better than me. But I can tell you one thing, death doesn't heal."

BILLIE

WHEN BILLIE SEES HER UNCLE THE NEXT DAY, THE WIND IS AN OCEAN, vast and crashing down with rushing pink blossoms. On the opposite end of his balcony, a man in a wheelchair with James Brown hair gives her a salute, which she returns. For a time, he watches her expectantly, then together they watch the red and white gas station across the two-lane road.

Her uncle is inside making chicory coffee and not saying much. She's avoided delicate subjects like how long could she have possibly hid out in a closet and why hasn't she come here years sooner. He could have been like a second father. They'd joke and have favorite meals, he'd visit her in Philly. She'd have gotten a place with a guest room or at least a couch with a pullout bed. Maybe she would have had fewer mediocre boyfriends with pleasurably normal families.

Across the street, a girl at the gas station drops a bag

of ice. It smashes open, glittering over the asphalt. The girl kicks the bag, then stoops to shovel the loose ice back into the torn plastic, finally tossing the broken bag into a trunk with a dragging bumper.

Down in the scaled parking lot, a silver pickup truck pulls up and the middle-aged woman who gets out slaps and curses a pigtailed little girl standing at her feet. A doubtful older man in a wrinkled Yankees cap gets slowly out of the driver's seat. He leaves the truck door open and stands gazing into the gearbox as the little girl wails.

Billie slides along the rail toward the stairs. James Brown raises an eyebrow as she nears the top step. But as if she can feel Billie deliberating, the woman in the parking lot looks up: wearied, outraged, sheepish. Then the woman pushes the little girl inside one of the apartments. The older man in the Yankees cap still stares into the truck, as if doubting the reality of the seat.

"You making friends?" Her uncle is behind her shaking a cigarette from a flattened pack. He hands her a cup of coffee.

"I've never been popular." Billie sits down with the cup on his neighbor's small blue and white cooler, the backs of her thighs gluing themselves to the plastic lid. "Do you know that lady?"

"I seen her."

"And the little girl?"

"Maybe."

"Do you think that happens often?"

"If a child is disrespectful then they gonna get whupped.

Can't spare the rod. My momma didn't like to do it, but sometimes it had to be done."

"What about your father?"

"He only licked me once in a while when I'd been real bad. If he was around and could find me. Your daddy always said I got off easy being the baby of the family."

"But there is a difference between spanking and beating."

He lights his cigarette. "How often you get spanked?"

"What I'm saying is that it instills fear not respect."

"How often?" He inhales.

"My mother didn't believe in spanking."

He laughs. "Ain't she learn nothing from her time here in Mississippi?"

"Doesn't mean I never got hit." Her mother had a boy-friend who hit her a couple times when her mother wasn't home. Not a slap across the thighs, but a bend over, pants down, and wait for the belt. It was the dread that made her hate him. Billie peels her legs from the cooler. "Why do people who hate kids have them?"

"That's one of them age-old questions," her uncle says, taking a drag on his cigarette. He waves to a man in a camo jacket with a long, thin blond braid walking up the steps.

She sips the coffee and sets it down. "Where did you meet Lacey?"

"Truck stop casino she work at."

"Are you sure you don't want the house?"

He smiles. "Don't worry about me. This"—he gestures to the building—"is a temporary situation. I tell you what, nobody in here better off than me. I got a job and the place all to myself. There's five, six people living in some of these rooms. Not only that but I finished high school and did a year of college at Jackson State."

"Why did you stop?"

"I got offered a job at John Deere and went for the money. To be honest with you, I wasn't all that interested in school. I just knew Cliff was interested in me being interested."

Her uncle points down to a dark cherry Buick in the parking lot whose back window is covered with a trash bag. "That's my baby." He hands her a set of keys.

"You want me to drive?"

"I got one of my headaches."

"Have you taken anything?"

He waves this aside. "I got a prescription. But it don't seem to matter what I do. They come when they want."

"What does your doctor say?"

"That it could be any number of things."

"I think you need a second opinion." Maybe if they get to know each other, she can help him find a better doctor.

The air in the car is thick with canned heat. She dials up the AC, backing out of the spot so that they're facing the two-lane road. He turns off the AC and rolls down his window, looking older than he did the other night. "It don't work. Take a right out of the parking lot."

With the windows down, the hot wind rolls into them, burning and cooling. The sky above them is aching with rain. They drive behind a truck with an Ole Miss license plate and a large crucifix hanging off the rearview mirror. As the town is pulled behind them, the landscape becomes lush and stark. Brilliantly green with a few battered shacks half swallowed by a thicket.

When the car crackles down a dirt road, they roll up the windows. They slide in and out of wet patches as dust coats the windshield. For the first time in her life, Billie wishes she had a truck.

Avalon sits alone in the middle of a soybean field. She parks and opens the door, but her uncle doesn't move.

"I ain't even drove by here in a good while." His face is turned from her.

"You don't have to come in."

"I'll join you in a minute."

She gets out and walks up to a broken bottle tree guarding the scarred patchwork of wood and tin. Bottle trees are meant to trap bad spirits, but it looks like these ones got out. She tests the narrow set of stairs with a foot, then shakes the railing, glancing back. She can't see her uncle through the glare on the windshield.

Inside the air is dazed with heat. She can't walk too far because the roof is caving in at the back. There are still scraps of posters on the walls and the low wooden beams are twined with rows of burned-out Christmas lights. On the rotting floorboards is the naked stain of where a jukebox once sat near the plywood stage, and above the bar, the squiggle of a broken neon sign.

She sits on an uprooted church pew, her feet at the shattered cavern of a TV. She takes out her father's first book of poetry, *Race Records,* and flips to "Song 33."

SONG 33

My love,
We made our own island:

On soil too long blood fed
Where the wind don't come
Our wooden conjure stood
all night long.

There you hear the voice of
three hundred years of sweat,
there ride on sweet mercy
all night long.

No it ain't Paradise
It's only Avalon.
Feels like living longer,
But my love, we dying
all night long.

What does that last stanza mean? Why *dying*? The floor
creaks. Uncle Dee. He bends to pick a thread of tinsel from
the floor.

"My Grandmomma Ida used to call it devil's music.
Sure could call the devil up."

"I bet. Did my mom ever come here?"

"Only one time I can remember. She was carrying you.
But she was still a real good dancer." He twists the tinsel
between thumb and forefinger. "In them days this was the
place." He pokes at a ripped vinyl chair, then sits. "Used to

have a disco ball hanging right up there." He points to a beam, then leans back in the chair, cocking the front legs. "You play chess?"

"A little bit."

"Next time you come by the apartment we can play."

"The night my father died." She hesitates, afraid of her words in this air. "Did he come in here?"

"He stopped by."

"Where was I?"

"With your Grandmomma Ruby."

"How did he seem to you that night?" Suicide by fall doesn't really work unless it's off a bridge, but what if it was a kind of letting go, a spiraling down that ended in an accident?

He tosses the tinsel over his shoulder. "I don't know. He was him. Your daddy was the type of dude that ain't ever want to sit still. Didn't even like going to sleep. Said it was a waste of his time. When he was a kid he used to sometimes climb out of the window at night. Momma called it helling around."

"Where did he go?"

"Meet up with other boys, his little friends, maybe drink a little bit of that corn liquor, you know. Or he went out to be by hisself. Rampaging he called it. Just wandering around the woods and shit, talking to the trees."

"Wasn't he scared of snakes or running into the Klan?"

"He said he knew the barn where they met." Her uncle begins to pick bits of vinyl off of the seat between his legs. "Mama was real proud of him. She ain't learn how to read till she was an old woman. She wanted to read the Bible and my brother's poetry. Those were her motivations. But she didn't like no cussing or anything disrespectful, so there was a lot she would not read. I tried reading his play to her, but that was too much. I remember Cliff wanted me to come to New York and see it performed, but at the time I was too busy being foolish over a girl." He lets out a chuckle. "I spent the money he sent me for a bus ticket on her. Made her happy, but boy, he was mad. He call me up and say he ain't ever gonna give me even a quarter again.

"Now Momma liked that one poem—what was it called? 'My Sinful Days.' She like the hoping and preaching. No profanity, just redemption talk. She figure he wrote it for her. Maybe he did. I don't know.

"When he died, she was the one to go over and identify the body. I told her I would, but I hadn't turned eighteen. Still had another month. She went with my uncles, Floyd and John. Those were her big brothers. After that, she read over that poem a whole lot. Like it had answers." He looks down at the mess of vinyl on the floor. "She kept praying on it till she died. None of us understood why he had to go like that." He looks up at her. "So young, I mean. But I moved on from it all a long time ago. Had to."

"I understand."

"Way I see it, they ain't no point in dragging up something happen thirty years ago when I'm trying to make it through today."

Billie looks at her uncle sitting in the remains of Avalon. This place reminds her of a low tide when the sea has been sucked out and the skeletons of the deep are on display. He is like something left behind that was once alive, moving in shameless beauty, cold-blooded and innocent, concerned primarily with courtship.

"Lola came to see me."

He looks at her.

"Did you tell Lola's nana that I didn't want to see anybody?"

He frowns. "I said not to overwhelm you since this was your first time back. I know you want to talk more about Cliff's accident." His eyes are on the floor. "But I can't hardly talk about it to this day."

"I don't want to hurt you. But I do wish I knew more of what happened. What he was doing out there, what I was doing."

He looks at her. "You don't remember nothing?"

She shrugs. "I was asleep, I guess."

He bends forward, rubbing his temples. "Well, baby, you in the right place cause nobody round here remembers anything either."

AVALON

THIS HOUSE WAS ONCE A HOUSE. SEEN A GIRL MADE A MOTHER, A BOY become a father who come and go, come and go. Seen a son work the land, the land flood and ruin him and the bodies floating in it. Seen a woman rush home to check on her loose children, a white boy close by her side, another kind of son, devoted for now to his mighty black mother. Seen a child burned by a pot of boiling water on the stove. Seen these walls newspapered to keep out the cold.

Heard children singing, laughing, running into the sun to chase a bullfrog. Heard a baby offer up a word for the first time. Heard the silence after underwater drinking, and the fishhook whine of hunger from a small belly. Heard the knock of white men looking for a boy hiding at his uncle's house, heard shots in the night, far off but always too close, and heard weeping, too much weeping too damn much of the time.

Once there was only the rumble of thunder, split of rain, pulse of locust, the sounds day makes turning over into night. I heard tell of an army of wretched people, hardly clothed, who cleared the brake and swamp and panther, who built and served and escaped only when they died. Their children came here to sweat out the demons that are carried in the body.

This girl she comes wanting to know about a night in 1972 when the Isley Brothers were panting paradise for their queens and the Detroit Emeralds were asking all those babies to let them take them into their arms. But what can these walls say? Listen, girl, everything you want to know is near, telling itself over again, the song is on repeat.

BILLIE

the messages, crafts what she might say, but can't seem to take the time. There is always something else she should be doing: an errand to run, a repair to arrange, something to read. It's like she's thirteen years old again on summer vacation—curling up with a book for a day, pausing to eat thick slices of bleached cheese while standing on one leg in front of the open fridge. Daddy's house as fort.

Work has called. Two messages asking if she will be back in time for an important meeting. Departmental reshuffling, a new initiative. They don't need her. And really who does? None of the calls feel urgent, necessary.

During the day, she drives around the county with a mind sun-dipped, thoughtless, and content. At night, the ghosts come back, speaking under cicadas. She paces the yard, her feet searching for the spot that will let her remember what she doesn't know, bobbing under the surface of her own mind.

In the absence of people, certain objects have become reassuring: the ticking of power lines, a collapsed barn drowning in purple blooms, clothes flapping dry on a wire, winking lights set in roadside cemeteries so cars don't run over the graves. On the morning of the third day, she turns down the drive leading to Jim McGee's white house.

She pulls in next to a white pickup in the driveway, cutting the engine, then pushing up her sunglasses. As soon as she steps from the car, she is swallowed by the wet heat. Ringing the doorbell over and over produces nothing but the drowsy bark of a dog. She should have called first. She glances back at the pickup. No bumper stickers; no gun rack exhibiting love of hunting or general shooting at things; no cross dangling from the rearview mirror gesturing to a belief in the soul. She steps off of the front step and squeezes through a gap in the hedges, cupping her hand to the living room window.

"Hello?" A bare-chested guy in jeans and a mesh trucker hat comes from around the corner of the house, gripping a dirty shovel.

She quickly backs out of the shrubs. "Sorry, I was trying to see if anyone was home."

"Ma'am, this is private property." He looks sternly at her. "It looked like you were fixing to break in."

"I saw the truck but nobody answered the door." If something happens, no one will hear her but the soybeans. "I came to see Jim McGee?" The guy seems about her age, maybe younger. "Are you one of his sons?"

"I'm Harlan McGee. His only son."

"I just inherited the house down the road. One of the old tenant houses out that way." She points, hopefully with authority. "I'm Billie James."

He squints at her. "You're a relative of Miss Ruby's?"

"She was my grandmother."

He grins. "Miss Ruby was one of my favorite people. She used to mind me when I was little. You're staying in that old place? That house must be rotting to pieces. Like most everything round here, I guess. Sorry if I came across as rude just then."

"No, it's okay. I shouldn't have done that."

"You plan on fixing up the house?"

"Nothing major. Just working on making it livable."

"Well, good to meet you." He sets down his shovel, then takes off his work gloves, and puts his hand out. "You're Mr. Dee's daughter?"

"Cliff, her older son." Sweat trickles down her ribs.

"Ah, I think he passed before I was born."

"How old are you?"

"Thirty-one."

"Yeah, you would've been a baby then."

They stand there, saying nothing, reliving adolescent etiquette. Harlan yanks at a T-shirt half tucked in his back pocket and pulls it on.

"My dad's not here right now. Is there something I can help you with?" He lifts his hat and smooths back his damp hair. It's a sort of dirty honey color.

"Have you guys had any trouble with stealing out here?"

"Someone break into your car?"

"I mean like someone prowling around the house."

"Not in years far as I can remember." Sweat is already soaking through his shirt. "Someone bothering you?"

Should she tell him about the lights? Seems silly now.

"It could be some kids looking to party out by the creek," he says. "You should call my dad if anybody bugs you. I can give you his number."

"My uncle already gave it to me." She slaps a mosquito feasting on her calf.

"How long you planning on staying out there?"

"A few more days." She licks her thumb and rubs the bloody mark off. "I have my dog."

"I'll give you my number too, and you can holler at me in case my dad doesn't answer."

"That's generous of you but—"

"You got a piece of paper?"

At the car, she takes a pen and torn envelope from her bag and hands it to him.

"I'd invite you in"—he leans on the car to write, pausing to itch his stubble—"but I've got to hurry and clean up before I go to work."

"Where do you work?"

"A hospice just north of town."

"You're a nurse?" Ever since her mother's death, she's had a soft spot for nurses.

"No, though I have been thinking of going back to school for it." He hands her the paper. "I'm basically the cleanup crew. I make coffee, change beds. Sometimes I hold people's hands."

"It must be hard to work there."

"Some days it is, when a bunch of patients die in a row. But we all feel down when that happens. The chaplain says to try to think of it as an honor to be part of their journey." He clears his throat then wipes his hair back again. "I worked at a catfish plant before, but this pays better."

She looks up at the white house. "Do you know how long my grandmother worked here?"

"Well, my granddaddy built this place in the thirties, but we owned the land awhile before—"

"So you're old money."

"I don't think the family is what it was in his day. I couldn't say when Miss Ruby started working here. That's a good question for my dad. I remember Miss Ruby used to take care of the laundry and dinner and minding me. And that she was the sweetest, best-hearted lady, and the most forgiving. She passed when I was about six or seven. Did you come to the funeral? We might have met there as kids."

"No." Billie folds the paper into a tiny square. It's not his fault that he's spent more time with her grandmother than she has. Or that her grandmother lived in poverty despite decades of hard work. Or that someday, like his father, he will own the land where her father is buried. She pushes the paper deep into her pocket. "Hey, do you know where I would get those plugs for bugs?"

"Bug plugs?" He laughs.

"Okay, that sounds weird. I mean the electric plug things that are supposed to kill bugs."

"Pest repellers? Walmart I guess. Or the hardware store

downtown. Here." He hands her back the pen. "My dad's retired now so he's around pretty often. You might want to call over here tomorrow morning."

"Thanks for your help."

She gets in the car. They smile at each other through the glass, between the weight of time and heat. His eyes are blue. This whole time she thought they were brown.

Billie backs out to the end of the drive, stopping to look up at the white house. She has been here before.

BILLIE HAS FIVE DREAMS THAT NICHT ALL SET IN HER FATHER'S house. But it isn't his house, it is somewhere else where the rooms spread into one another. In three of those dreams, the house has a basement, though she never goes down but stands in the doorway, hovering above the steps, waiting for what will come up out of the dark.

Rufus's nails clip across the room and Billie lifts her head. He noses her feet, wanting to go out. She grabs her phone—it's late. She pulls on shorts and lets him out front. In the kitchen, she brews coffee and pours the last of her cereal into a plastic cup, mixing in creamer and a little water. She eats a spoonful and spits it in the trash, then dumps the rest. The creamer must have gone bad, unless there's something wrong with the water. It doesn't matter. She's leaving tomorrow, stopping by the cemetery to visit her father's grave, then driving the first leg to Knoxville. Today is the day she must call Jim McGee, once she gets up the nerve.

The house no longer feels sinister like it's harboring a subterranean lair. She sits in Sheila's chair, drinking her coffee black, staring up at tufts of old cobwebs wound around nails in the ceiling. The living room is littered with the contents of the three boxes of her mother's things from Gran's storage unit: newspaper clippings, old records, a program from the National Women's Political Caucus in 1973, her baby book, a postcard from Memphis with Elvis in uniform sitting in the kitchen with his gaunt parents, her mother's first and only book, *Those Who Drank Gold,* as well as her heavily underlined favorites: Marc Bloch's *Feudal Society;* Hanawalt's *The Ties That Bound: Peasant Families in Medieval England;* Tuchman's *A Distant Mirror: The Calamitous 14th Century;* and two books by Carlo Ginzburg with killer titles: *The Cheese and the Worms: The Cosmos of a Sixteenth-Century Miller* and *The Night Battles: Witchcraft and Agrarian Cults in the Sixteenth and Seventeenth Centuries,* and even a couple of Billie's old books—*Flowers in the Attic* and *Summer of My German Soldier*—slipped in. Her father's out-of-print books are near the door: his two books of poetry, *Race Records* and *Flatbottom Unrest,* a random poetry anthology he coedited, and his play *Hellhound.*

Out on the porch, she sits on a towel with her mother's book, subconsciously keeping count of how many noblemen die of anal fistulas. The book opens with a discussion of the number of peasant children who perished in fires from candles catching on their straw mats or drowned in a ditch. Why were there so many ditches in fourteenth-century England? There's a memento mori illustration on the first page: a skeleton Death grabbing the arm of its next victim—an unwilling nobleman in a poufy hat. *Remember that you have to die.* Like living with her mother you could ever forget.

Instead of calling Jim McGee, she reads a chapter on

Henry II of France's childhood where his father, King Francis, is captured during a battle against the Holy Roman Emperor, Charles V, and King Francis offers up his two oldest sons, little Henry and his elder brother, Francis, to take his place in Spain while he supposedly pays off the ransom. The boys are six and seven. They are imprisoned for over three years.

"As a result," her mother writes, "Henry developed a brooding, solitary nature and a deep attachment to the ideals of chivalric romance. At sixteen, he acquired a thirty-five-year-old mistress, Diane de Poiters." But he never outgrows her. Diane remains Henry's mistress into her fifties, though not without some contrivance. She carefully cultivates her own physical beauty, dressing in her signature black and white; she lets him have a few lesser mistresses from time to time; and she encourages him to procreate with his wife, the queen, and instructs the poor woman on how to do it right. When Henry dies in a jousting accident, getting a lance through the eye, the queen, a potato-faced, razor-sharp Medici, kills the eye gouger and tosses out the mistress.

Her bookmark is a Polaroid of her parents. In it, her petite mother is wearing a sort of minicaftan, her face naked without her glasses, her blond hair loose and center parted. Her father stands a foot taller, smiling closemouthed in sunglasses, a white shirt, and jeans, his arm around her waist. They look at the camera like they know what each other are thinking.

Billie puts down the book, looking out at the green spill of depopulated land. She lies back in the sun, knees up, just resting her eyes. She wakes to find Rufus curled next to her and her phone ringing. She reaches for it and knocks it off the porch. Whatever. Inside she brews more coffee, then squats in the living room and flips through the dusty records: Charlie Parker, Aretha Franklin, Ida Cox, Sara Martin's "Death Sting Me Blues"—it feels like the Sara Martin record is missing. She shakes the album and a wad of typed pages drops to the floor.

CHAPTER 2—YOUNG THING BRIGHT

In 1961, the day I found out that the first Freedom Riders numbered only thirteen people, I dropped out of college and ran like hell to the SNCC office to sign myself up. Not only was this my calling, but it was *the* calling I decided. Lucky for me, I was too naïve then to really think about what it meant to be stepping on one of these buses.

It would be the first time I had been back in Mississippi since I left for school. I was scared, petrified, ready to piss my pants as many a man has done in the moment before battle. But this was my war and I knew it. I sat on the bus squarely between the mandated black section and the established white, both hands gripping my thighs because when I set them on the seat in front of me, they shook. Driving north along Lake Pontchartrain, I wondered if it was fate that the river near my hometown was the Yazoo, which happens to mean the River of Death.

I passed the time by looking out of the window and counting telephone poles, but there was no escape from the dread.

After what felt like years, we finally pulled into town and went by columned banks imitating the Greeks. By then, I was hoping some mythic quality from my childhood daydreams might rub off on me, and that if I didn't live past today I could be someone folks would sing about. Nearing the courthouse, going past the Confederate monument, I spotted the mob. We all looked at one another on that bus as if to say: You are mine and if your blood should spill, I will feel it.

As the bus made a wide turn, I pushed down my porkpie hat and prayed that my moral intention would cohere with my future conduct. Or if only for fifteen minutes my body would not betray me. The others around me—rabbis, barbers, students— were mostly "veterans" of the Movement and my age and color. But we suddenly seemed too small, even though that was what had first inspired me to join. And now that I was home in Mississippi, seeing the hissing, spitting crowd wielding clubs and bats, I knew how much I had never been welcome.

When we stopped, there were shouts and howls, the sides of the bus being beaten in the name of Tradition. We stood and filed into the aisles with the hush of priests. My stomach cut itself open and acid filled my mouth. I was in the other theater of the blues. I was as close as I could ever come to being like Jesus.

As I walked the length of the bus, I heard every step of my shoes down that aisle and the early afternoon took on the mantle of deep night. At the stairwell, I looked out onto savage faces who longed to take something, someone, me into their hands. But someone took my hand, somebody else began to sing. And for maybe thirty seconds, I was living philosophy.

Once I stepped onto the road I took a hit right to the face. My eyes and nose broke open and ran into my shirt. Everything burned. I went maybe two more steps when a man with a lead pipe cracked my thigh. At first, I wanted to run. But as I backed away, I realized that a couple of people—our people—were getting through the crowd and making it to the station doors. So I picked up my head (I had long since lost my hat) and tried to join them. When I rushed forward, I saw that one of the girls, the only white girl of our group, Pia, had been knocked to the ground. A group of men had surrounded her, one kicking her in the stomach. The mob had a special kind of rage for those riders who were white. I pushed my way over and dragged her up by the shoulders. Until then, I don't believe I'd ever touched a white woman, let alone held one in my arms, but the smile she gave me was pure and sweet as honey. We limped through the mob, taking our licks together until we stepped into the bus station and through to the white portion of the waiting room. Three minutes later, we no-good troublemaking lawless Commie agitators were being cuffed and loaded into the paddy wagon heading off to jail.

In three years we would be back in Mississippi for a longer and deadlier siege, but I didn't know that yet. Nor did I know how important Pia would come to be in my life.

Holy Shit. Billie covers her face with both hands. She reads again. It's him.

She inspects inside each and every record, finding nothing. But this is him, this is Daddy speaking, this is unpublished, unread, unseen words direct from Clifton James. This is . . . Chapter 2. Where's Chapter 1?

She stands, whoops, jumps, and runs into the yard for her phone. Who to call? Uncle Dee? Jude? But what if for some weird reason Uncle Dee doesn't want to publish it? He's the literary executor, not her. And this isn't fiction, it's her mother meeting her father, and maybe the rest covers less savory parts of his life. Maybe Uncle Dee is the one who has the other chapter. Would he admit it if she asked? She goes back inside and throws herself into Sheila's chair. If only one of the ghosts around here would tell her what to do.

There's always the Good Doctor, as her mother used to call him, though of course Mom was being facetious. Dr. Melvin Hurley (B.A. University of North Carolina, M.A. University of Massachusetts at Amherst, Ph.D. University

of Chicago) (primary research areas: African American literature and social history in the nineteenth and twentieth
centuries, emphasis on black radical movements) (author
of *The Long Dispossession: The Counter-Reconstruction)* (Dis-
sertation: "The Diaspora of Memory: The Violent Resurrection of the Surreal in the Poetry of Clifton James") has been
working on the only biography of her father for ten thousand
years. This book, tentatively entitled *The Prophet of Avalon,*
is a book that will place her father (according to Hurley's
faculty page) on "the pantheon of black genius."

Maybe she could leak its existence to him first, in case
her uncle disappears it once she hands it over. But her mother
did always seem to despise Hurley, probably hating the role
of Artist's Wife/Helpmeet/Muse. As far as Billie knows there
is no one else interested in her father's work; certainly no
other scholar has ever contacted her about him. Though why
would the chapter be in her mother's stuff? Jude said her
father pretended the decision to divorce was mutual, but it
wasn't. He wanted to move back to Mississippi and he didn't
want her mother coming with him.

After e-mailing Dr. Hurley from the library, Billie follows a log truck to a restaurant in the next town over, passing a record number of unrepaired cars with crushed hoods
along the way. She walks through a glass foyer lined with
community magazines and old Mardi Gras beads. Two construction workers coming out smile at her. She forgot to put
on a bra. Turns out the restaurant is freezing and the corn
bread is bad.

In the booth behind her, a man with a silver-brown
ponytail and blue coveralls devours a chicken-fried steak.

He's loud on his phone but she doesn't mind because it makes the place feel less deserted. She orders sweet tea and coffee, plays with her bendy straw as she reads the chapter again and again. The chicken-steak man gets up to go to the bathroom, leading with his belly. There are bits of corn bread in her hair. At least she brushed her teeth. She shakes out her hair and picks up her mug. The coffee is thick and cold as eels, a medieval delicacy.

Her phone rings. An unfamiliar number.

"Hello, is this Miss James? This is Dr. Hurley."

She smiles at the chicken-steak man as he comes back. Looks like she won't be leaving tomorrow after all. She wants to know all the stories of Greendale's abandoned houses, secret affairs, and ruinous personal wars.

LOLA

HE ACTED SURPRISED WHEN SHE BROUGHT UP THE WOMAN'S NAME.
Not surprised-scared, more like surprised what's-the-big-deal.
Like he had nothing to hide. Lola relaxed about it while they
were talking, but now that she's on her way down to Mississippi, she's suspicious again. Some men lie so good they fool
themselves into thinking that they did nothing wrong.

Yes, she wanted to come back down for Billie, but it was
also the perfect excuse to leave town. *My cousin needs me.*
And she needs Billie to keep her from doing something stupid in this damn stupid relationship.

Billie takes their tray of tamales from the counter, laughing with Cedric, the owner, who Lola has known since she
was a baby. Billie sits down across from Lola all smiles. "He
promises me that these are the best tamales in town."

"Best in the state." Lola takes her plate from the tray.

"You been listening to me go on about my man all morning. What about you?"

"Wait. How spicy are these?"

"Just try it. Are you seeing someone?"

"No." Billie chews ice from her cup. "I'll probably end up alone."

"If those are your table manners. And you're fine with that?" Lola peels the foil back from her tamales. "Now these are beautiful."

"My mother was a bachelor."

Lola unwraps the glistening corn husk. "You mean single?"

"I prefer the term *bachelor*. Do I eat it with my hands or fork?"

"If you don't want to get messy, use a fork. Or you could scoop it on a cracker. Here." Lola tosses a packet of crackers onto Billie's tray. "You want kids?"

Billie cuts the tamale with a fork. "I like kids. But I don't get that baby feeling, you know?"

"But what if you fall in love?"

Billie finishes chewing. "Oh god, you're so cheesy. Sure, I could fall in love. I mean I have, or I thought I did once. Are you in love with your guy?"

"I don't know. What, you got something to say about that?"

"He stresses you out."

Lola wipes her fingers on a napkin. Maybe there's some truth to that. "He's so relaxed."

"Too relaxed."

"Right? It's like he likes hanging out with me, but it's not that necessary."

"Not love then." Billie crumples the foil of her wrapper into a ball and tosses it into the nearest trash can. "Swish."

Lola sips her Coke. "You are a child. I am having lunch with a seven-year-old."

"Being a bachelor doesn't mean celibacy."

"Tell me who he is right this minute."

Billie looks up toward the counter where Cedric is helping another customer. "He's white."

"A white guy from around here? Oh no you— Oh shit."

"Now I'm not going to tell you anything."

"Nobody gonna hear us over Al Green. Cedric must be going deaf. My mind is saying one word and one word only: *no*."

"Calm down, nothing's happened."

"But you planning on it."

"I am not."

"Who is it?"

"Why does it matter?"

"I might know him."

"You don't. He's younger."

"Even worse."

"You're not making me want to confide in you."

"Look, I have no issue with interracial relationships, but they don't last, not around here. It's too much pressure."

Billie gets up and grabs more napkins. "Plenty of marriages don't last." She sits. "The divorce rate is like sixty percent."

"He ain't never gonna get over how his mother treats you."

"I'm not marrying anybody."

"I ain't getting up until you tell me who it is."

Billie rolls her eyes. "Fine. You can't tell anyone. Swear."

"I swear." They shake pinkies.

"It's Mr. McGee's son."

"So either you decided to crush on the worst person you could find or the nearest. Billie, you don't want to get with the great-great-grandson of the man who raped your great-great-grandmother."

Billie puts down her last tamale. "Okay, I think I'm finished eating."

Lola stands. "Man, I'm gonna need to do an extra day of cardio now."

In the car, Billie says nothing as they pull out of the parking lot. Lola glances at her. "What is it?"

"I found something my father wrote."

"What?" Lola pulls over, a tire bumping the sidewalk. "What was it?"

"I think it's part of a memoir."

"That's fantastic." Lola puts the car in park. "So what's the issue?"

Billie stares into the windshield. "I don't know if I should give it to Uncle Dee. I mean, he's the literary executor; he's the one who legally can say what happens to it."

Lola presses on the hazard lights. "But you don't trust him."

"It's not that. He's been as up front with me as he can. But it's painful for him. So I've done something kind of underhanded—I contacted this scholar who specializes in my father's work and he's going to come down here and look at it and maybe even try to help me find the rest."

"This is like some spy shit."

"Am I a bad person?"

"Listen to me, I love Dee but I ain't be trusting him." Lola pulls back onto the road. "All you need to know is you can't get caught up with that white family."

BILLIE

IN CELEBRATION OF HER FIND, SHE DRIVES TO WALMART AND BUYS the cheapest bike she sees. There's no reason that she can't do at least one of the things she's been avoiding.

The sunwarm gates to the cemetery are shut. Billie steps through the wide bars of the iron fence where a massive oak bows, its branches touching down in the middle of the grass. There are a couple rows of lacquered, mold-spattered graves then an older section where headstones lean against one another, half of them underwater from the last heavy rain. The world outside of the cemetery gates bends in the dizzy heat.

Among the anthills, the Willies, the Hatties, and the Maes, she finds her father. He lies between Mose and Oz; one who is Only Sleeping, and the other who died in World War II. She crouches so that she can trace his name with her finger. CLIFTON SILAS JAMES 1940–1972.

"Hi, Daddy." Around her the shadows of the trees move as if directed by the saccharine clatter of birds. "I wish you could see me." Already her eyes sting. "Even if I haven't made very much of myself." She smiles, wiping wet grass from her knee. "But maybe if I strike it rich, I can buy this cemetery from the McGees."

A warm wind makes the trees drop their fronds onto the soaked earth. A few raindrops hit her shoulder. Billie stands and looks up; a corner of the sky is matted black with clouds. After pulling some weeds and brushing away leaves, she lays flowers on the mud under his headstone. It's something. A beginning.

Billie rides up the two-lane road and away from the cemetery. There's a conference call for work tomorrow that she needs to prep for. A man is leaning on a white truck in a church parking lot, the tattoo of a chained dog on his arm.

"Hey," the guy calls as he spots her. The face under the camo hat is too small for his smile.

She nods, smiling faintly. She should have brought Rufus. The guy takes off his hat and wipes his buzzed, angular head, staring until she can feel the press of him. He has the look of a man who has had something gone bad inside: a miasma, an evil smell thought to cause the Black Death, a rot that corrupted the air. Maybe she should wear one of those terrifying medieval bird masks to ward off guys like him, a prehistoric beak stuffed with flowers and herbs.

"You gotta be careful out here alone," the guy calls from behind her.

No cars or people around as usual. She pedals faster, turning off the two-lane road as soon as she can and cutting through the parking lot of a shack selling CB radios, heading for a busier road that she knows has houses down it. As she glances back, her bike slips on the gravel and she is skidding sideways, gravity peeling her fingers back from the handlebars. Her thigh slams into the ground, scraping the skin below her shorts and filling it with dirt, the bike pinning her down in the middle of the lot.

She lies stunned under the frame. She tries to push herself up, but her palms are pitted with rocks, so she eases onto her peeling forearms studded with blood. Hot tears stream down her cheeks like she's eight years old, hobbling home for her mother.

It starts to rain. Hot spatterings at first, then long warm drops. Half of the sky so dark it's almost green. A color that is telling her something. She sits, spitting into the bottom of her shirt and dabbing it on her stinging hands and knees. She picks up the bike, but the damn chain won't go back on. That guy better not come looking for her like guys like him sometimes do.

She continues on her circuitous route; eventually this road will connect to hers, and then she will lock herself in the house and not come out. There's an unpaved county road that's faster, but it will turn to mud in the rain and is dotted with forgotten houses. In the dirt between asphalt and field, she steps over mangled bits of plastic, a few beer bottles, and an old tin of dip. The first house she passes has a dog chained to a tree and the next has bits of torn furniture that have failed to dissolve on the lawn. Squirrels hop and slink through its clotted trash. A woman is standing barefoot next to a boy and little girl on the porch. When they see her, they huddle back, the woman hiding in the doorway as the boy grabs the little girl by the hand.

It isn't until she's already passed the house that she looks back to find a teenage boy, shirt off, lounging on a metal chair in the middle of the lawn. He is looking in her direction but doesn't seem to see her. He is sitting so still that he is part of the yard. Though the windows are covered with plywood and cardboard, she feels she is being watched.

On a flat stretch of road along a field, a white truck passes her, brakes, then starts making a U-turn. Better not be that guy. As the truck turns, she drags the bike off the shoulder and into the plowed field turning to mud from the rain. She could run across it, but there's nothing beyond this field but another one. The truck is coming her way. She quickly kneels, trying to jam the chain back on. Riding would be better than running. Maybe it's just somebody turning around. Fuck it. She throws down the bike and runs.

The truck revs up to her, the passenger window going down. The driver leans over. "Need a ride?"

HE PUTS HER BIKE IN THE BACK, AND WHEN HE GETS IN THE CAB, reaches over and squeezes her fingers, then puts the truck in drive. She leaves her hand where he squeezed it, admiring her wrist's innocence. To escape the tornado, they drive south for a drink. Billie tells Harlan how she fell trying to get away from the creepy guy in the church parking lot. She likes that he believes her, no questions asked.

On the way to the bar, they pass a church billboard: HONK IF U LOVE JESUS/TEXT IF U WANT TO MEET HIM.

"Have you ever texted?" she asks.

"No." He slows and honks.

"A believer, huhn?" A couple of crushed empty beer cans keep sliding into her feet.

"It was a big part of my upbringing."

"But then wouldn't you want to meet him?"

"Already have." He dials down the radio. "You got pretty banged up." He gestures at her legs, the gashes filling with stinging blood. "I got a first aid kit in the back."

"I need a drink more than gauze right now," she says. "Besides, I'll have to shower to wash all the dirt out."

"Are you big into bike riding?"

She laughs. "I haven't ridden a bike in years. I bought it because I've been sitting on my ass reading and eating cheese. Maybe I should've brought my gun to ride my bike, but I didn't know where to put it."

"He probably wasn't going to do nothing but be a jackass."

"You never know what kind of childhood he had."

He rolls his eyes.

"What? Too bleeding heart for you?"

He lifts a hand from the wheel to concede. "Maybe I shouldn't judge cause I had a pretty good childhood, but if somebody's an adult then there are consequences for their choices."

"Sure, but there are crimes committed out of ignorance and deprivation and suffering, and then there's actual evil people who are sociopathic narcissists. Shouldn't you be preaching to me about forgiveness and redemption? You forgive not seven times but seven times a hundred."

"Seventy times seven," he says.

"I was close."

"You seem to know the Bible for someone who isn't a Christian."

"My mother was an academic. She specialized in Christian medieval theology. So I know me some King James." She inspects her raw elbow. "My cousin is in jail. I hate thinking of him in there. He was such a sweetheart."

"What's he in for?"

"Weed. I think possession with intent to sell."

"That's too bad."

"Yeah, if he was white he wouldn't be in there."

SHE WOULD NEVER COME HERE ON HER OWN. WHITE BOYS TOO YOUNG to be smoking are out front with their dirt bikes crowded around a beat-up car. There's one girl, maybe fourteen, in flip-flops and too much eye makeup, smoking a menthol next to a cobwebbed grill in the middle of the yard. Billie follows Harlan into the double-wide trailer through a doorway wreathed with tiny American flags. Inside is dark and the AC is blasting. Beneath everything is the rotten apple stink of old beer. She is the only woman except for a blond bartender, bending over rinsing glasses at the far end of the bar.

Harlan orders whiskeys while Billie goes to the bathroom and tries to wash the grit from her hands and knees using pink industrial soap and brown paper towels. She comes out smelling like second grade, of a tiny elementary school in Utah outside of Ogden where she was set adrift in a sea of Mormons. Her mother used to let her ride in the truck bed of their blue pickup when she dropped her off. Once she was climbing out and she fell, losing a loose tooth to the ice.

She slips quickly into their booth, happy to hide from all

the eyes she's getting because she's brown, or a stranger, or a woman. She raises her whiskey. "To you not running me over."

He clinks her glass. "I am a gentleman." He drinks then says, "I figured you'd have left town by now."

"I was going to, but I've decided to stay a little longer."

"Any reason in particular?"

"I can't say yet. I don't want to jinx it. Let's talk about you. Are you married?"

He smiles, a real smile with teeth. "Haven't gotten around to that. I almost did with my ex. We talked about flying to Vegas the first month we were dating. She's never been out of Mississippi except to go to the casino in Baton Rouge and Panama City."

"Panama?" There are these little rocks she can't get out of her hand.

"Florida. There's a pretty beach there. Beautiful clear blue water, white sands. I prefer Destin though. We've got a kid, a little boy who's five. Tyler. He's basically the center of my life right now."

"Are things rough?"

"It's mostly all right." He drinks his whiskey. "But man, when we first broke up and she wouldn't let me see the baby—I'd be driving to work, going along like normal, and it would just seize me up. I tried to get her to do counseling, but she wouldn't. She doesn't want to know why she does what she does." He picks at a groove in the table with the bottom of his glass. "Enough of me. You ever had your heart broken?"

"I'm not drunk enough to answer that question."

"C'mon," he says, smiling again.

"Of course. But I don't have a kid." She taps the ice in her whiskey with the cocktail straw. "My parents divorced when I was a baby. The good thing is I don't remember the fights."

"C'mon, what was your heartbreaker like?"

Every so often, a memory will come grasping. A stupid fight in the car for no reason. How her mother sat her up on the kitchen counter and took a jar of pickled onions from the fridge and ate one after another until they were gone. The tops of her mother's hands mottled brown from the IVs.

"I guess time heals all wounds," he says.

"Does it?" Her knees are burning from the cleaning. "I think that's inaccurate." Their glasses are near empty. She gets up. "I'll get the next round."

While she's at the bar, Harlan goes to the men's room. Next to her, an older man in a squashed baseball cap smiles from his stool with an oily drunk look. "That your boyfriend?"

She considers for a split second. "Yes."

A country song comes on loud, a woman singing of a small town and something about a baby. Not as bad as the guy before, singing about young love and a fight.

"You like him?"

"What?" She glances at the man. Thin but the skin hanging off his face is fleshy. "Sure."

He tips on his stool to bring their faces closer. "You're real beautiful," he says.

"Thanks."

"Are you Mexican?"

"Nope." She lays her arm on the bar, ready to flag down the bartender, who is pouring at the other end.

He sits back. "I don't mind Mexicans working round here. I'm in favor of it. They ain't lazy."

She pulls her arm back in. "Who is?"

"They're hard workers."

"Who's lazy?"

"The problem is drugs. That's what brought on all the black-on-black crime. Before it was nothing like it is now."

"What about the white-on-white crime?" The blond bartender is coming over. Lacey. "Shit."

"You're real pretty. Is that out of bounds?" He eyes the men's room. "Don't tell him I said it."

Billie moves down the bar toward Lacey, whose expression reminds her of two big girls in eighth grade who used to try and pull out her hair. To see if it was real they said. That was when she knew life would be easier if she were blond, hairless, and white.

"What do you want?" Lacey says, leaning on the bar.

"Two whiskeys on the rocks. My uncle said you worked at a truck stop casino." Billie slides a twenty-dollar bill on the counter.

"I do."

Harlan reappears at the other end of the bar. Thankfully he stops to speak to two older men at a table.

"I went to high school with his ex." Lacey slices a lime then grabs a bottle of whiskey from the shelf behind her. "He went to a different academy than us. More expensive.

But he flunked out." Lacey pours the whiskey to the lip of the glass, her teal nails bright around the dark bottle. "Good thing you didn't go to school round here."

"Were the proms segregated?"

"Aren't you precious?" Clipping a slice of lime on the glass. "They don't have to be. By the time you get to high school things already are."

Harlan is still talking. One of the men pretends to punch him in the arm.

Lacey takes the money, opens the till, and counts out change. "A little bird told me they saw him partying with some girl just out of high school, don't think she's even eighteen. Now that's just tacky, ain't it?" She grabs her purse from a shelf under the till, takes out a compact to check her makeup. "I need to lay out more. Working nights has me looking like a vampire. Yeah, his family thought my friend was trash. They wanted him to be a lawyer but he turned out a fuckup, bless his heart. Your uncle better not find out y'all are dating."

"We're just friends."

Lacey's eyes meet hers. "The McGees have more photographs of your family than y'all do. That's fucked-up. Why're you gonna have more pictures of somebody else's family?"

"Because they're the ones that owned the cameras." Harlan is back in the booth. Billie lays out a tip. "Why are you with my uncle?"

"He ain't married, he don't have kids, and he don't play games." She doesn't touch the tip. "And he's funny."

"Don't people around here give you trouble?"

"My momma. Fifty dollars says she's got the ladies at

church praying for me to date a nice white Christian boy. But we don't hang out here, we go to his place or out of town, sometimes down to New Orleans."

"Well, if you actually care about him, don't make a big deal out of this." Billie picks up the glasses and heads back to the booth.

Harlan takes his drink from her, glancing up at the bar. "You know her?"

"No," she says, sitting down.

Her whiskey doesn't taste right. Something in the glass.

"I should go," she says.

"You just got our drinks."

"My knee hurts." Which is true but not.

ON THE DRIVE BACK, HIS TRUCK CUTS THROUGH THE DOWNTOWN neighborhoods and they pass a little black girl with braids sitting in a driveway, leaning against a brown car door. The house across from the girl is draped in Confederate flags. It even has one hoisted up a thick metal flagpole in the middle of the lawn. Every time she sees the state flag with its mini Confederate flag in the corner she double-takes. Lola says it's grief for what never was.

At the house, Rufus scuffles to the door. She goes in, catching his paws before they hit her sore thighs, and sets them down.

"Bad owner." She scratches his head and neck. "Poor puppy, poor boy." She opens the screen door to let him out. He bounds toward Harlan, who is walking up the drive.

She's been away too long. "Down, Rufus."

Harlan stops at the bottom of the steps. "Can I come

in?" Rufus is prancing at the backs of his legs. Harlan holds a hand out for him to sniff. "Hey, buddy."

It is tempting to latch the screen with the little hook screwed into the doorframe. Rufus abandons Harlan and rolls in the shorn yard, dead grass coating his back. Harlan's eyes meet hers through the mesh.

"That rolling means he needs a bath."

"Probably. I'll come out there," she says.

On the edge of the porch, he watches the field while she picks at the jagged edge of a fingernail. He turns to the woods behind them. "Do you know the names of these trees?"

"Of course not."

"That there's a pine."

"I know that one. I'm not stupid."

He hops down, holding out his hand. "C'mon."

She doesn't move. "Where?" She shouldn't care what he does or who with.

"To the woods."

"There's snakes."

"I bet there's plenty of cypress out by the creek. They're a real fascinating tree."

"I never would have guessed you were such a tree fa-natic."

"You should know what's on your property." He walks closer. "What's wrong?" He seems genuinely concerned.

"I'm tired." But she lets him pull her to her feet and calls to Rufus. "How did you know there was a creek behind the house?" If she walks behind Harlan, then he'll get bit first, and she won't be sucking out any poison.

"I've been out here a million times since I was a kid. I

don't know if you remember but Miss Ruby's stood about a mile that way." He points to his left. "It was torn down about twenty years ago. And the creek runs behind my folks' place too, just farther back."

Harlan shows her the bald cypress trees dotting the creek with their wide bottoms and flat green feathery branches. Rufus trots ahead until there is only the tinkle of his collar.

"I like the roots," she says. "Sort of like bubbles of wood coming out of the water."

"They're called knees. Cypress can live for a thousand years."

These trees know what happened. "My father died out here."

He looks at her.

"I don't mean right here in this spot," she says. "It could have been the front yard, I don't know." Maybe if Mr. McGee dies she could buy the cemetery off of Harlan.

"How did he die?"

"Your dad didn't tell you? They said it was an accident. He fell and hit his head and it sent him into a coma and he died."

"I'm sorry. That's hard, real hard. And here I was complaining about my ex."

"I don't think that one person's pain cancels out another's."

Back at the house, they sit on the back porch. The back door has a ladybug infestation. A crawling mass whirling over the screen during the day then vanishing at night.

She points to a tree beginning to bloom with clusters of purple flowers. "What's that one?"

Harlan picks a long blade of grass that she missed with the lawn mower. "A crepe myrtle."

"This is us just being friends, right?"

He looks away, nodding. It's hard to say more. To say this is all they can be, given their history, which began before them and may go on long after they're dead.

He ties the blade of grass into a knot. "If you're gonna stick around for a while, you need to teach Rufus not to go after snakes or he'll get bit in the face."

HARLAN

HE BARELY REMEMBERS DRIVING HOME BUT HERE HE IS IN THE PARK-
ing lot. He pulls the keys from the ignition and stares at the
still-glowing odometer. When she kicked off her boots, her
little ankles were freckled in mosquito bites. Weird how he
somehow finds that attractive but being into a pretty girl is
the most natural thing in the world. No harm in it. He gets
out and slams the door, walking through the poorly lit parking lot then across the bald square of grass at the center of
his apartment complex.

From the beginning he knew he shouldn't be messing
with her. Ain't he got enough on his plate trying to hold
on to his kid? But right when he thought she was gone, he
spotted her on the side of the road, struggling with that
crappy bike, all scraped up like a little kid. She needed him
to swoop in. But later in the yard, she spooked him when she

told him about her daddy's death; he felt like she was the one swooping in, prophesying something.

He unlocks the door. The apartment always looks bad because of the wall-to-wall tile floor. But it's what he could afford what with child support. He flops down on his parents' old couch, head next to a basket of unfolded laundry, and turns on the TV, tossing the remote. The game is on. Might as well let it play. He planned on coming home and cleaning up. Tomorrow is his night with Tyler. But he lays back and stares into the spackled ceiling, only glancing at the score twice, not remembering what it is either time.

At the fridge he grabs a beer. Just one left and he has a mind to head out for more. Maybe he's ready to do more than hook up, to start dating again. He tried right after Debbi, but nothing lasted. He needs someone who likes to go out and do things, be active. Someone who would actually get along with his family.

He lays back down on the couch with his head propped up. Maybe if they slept together he could get closure or something. He could stop thinking about Billie's beautiful smile—she almost has dimples. And her ass and her legs and what she'd look like under him.

She doesn't really look black, unless you know it and then you can see it. More like Hispanic. He had a crush on a black girl in fifth grade, Shonda, who would never even look at him except to make fun. He was sure Shonda felt something too, but neither of their daddies would have ever let them come home with the other. At his high school there was only one black student, a serious kid with glasses that he never saw speak, except in English class.

Now he ain't like some of the old folks round here. He didn't grow up believing in all that. His daddy, though he hated all the negative press on the town he was raised up in, did say that while he was living his life of hunting and clowning around, the blacks on the other side of town were living one very different. His daddy said that too many good people blamed the town's trouble on the blacks or rednecks and never took any responsibility on themselves. But he only spoke about it once when Harlan had come home for the weekend that first and only year at Ole Miss. His father had pulled some strings after he finally got his GED. They were sitting on the back porch, his father pouring bourbon like he was Faulkner. Harlan had felt like a real man out there discussing hard subjects in the dark with drinks in hand. But then like a little boy, marveling at the love he felt for his father and the rich land buzzing all around.

Harlan never had nothing against the shy black boy with glasses, even said what's up to him in the hall. His parents had been strict about being decent to everybody no matter if they were brown, white, or purple. But he has brought enough trouble on them. Enough heartache over Tyler and Debbi and her fucked-up family. They bailed him out when Debbi's brother stole a car while on probation and tried to fight him in a parking lot. Bought him the car seat and the stroller and the crib and pretty much everything for Tyler. He's never been able to explain to his dad as to why he did the things he did. His younger self seems like someone only faintly related to him. It's a mystery. He had thought he could change Debbi or save Debbi, but she was who she was even when she was ashamed of it. And now he is cursed spending his nights wondering where she is and in what condition and who she's left the baby with. Tyler loves his mama, but Harlan can see the distance growing in the child's eyes when Tyler sees her coming, and he will never forgive her for it.

So why think about a girl who doesn't even go to church. Whose people worked for his. Billie will go soon and he won't remember why he ever carried on about it.

DR. MELVIN HURLEY

HOW HE MUST APPEAR SO SHORTLY AFTER HIS FLIGHT AND THE TWO-
hour drive down from Memphis in his woefully creased
blazer, redolent of cinnamon gum. He could explain why he
has gained five pounds, why his coffee-stained slacks rise a
centimeter too high above his ankles, or why his briefcase is
bursting with boxes of assorted flavored toothpicks, or even
why, for example, he, a distinguished professor of English
and African American studies, could only concentrate on a
discarded issue of *Vogue* on the plane as opposed to reading
a particularly salient essay by one of his colleagues about
the way in which kinship was contested during the terror
of slavery. But the ubiquitous gerbil brain is something that
only another smoker could truly understand.

"Can I get you something to drink?" Billie flips the thick
braid, hanging half loose, over her shoulder. Cliff's daughter
is tall and disheveled, perhaps artfully so, her palms covered

in multiple Band-Aids and the thighs under her denim shorts raked with scabs.

She follows his gaze. "Biking accident," she says. "I have a little stick stain remover if you want it."

"Thank you, I"—he rubs at the coffee stain above his knee—"we hit some awful turbulence. I considered changing before I picked up the rental car, but I didn't want to be late."

"Oh, you should've called. It's not like I have anywhere to be. Coffee? Water? Beer? Whiskey?"

He stops rubbing. "Coffee would be perfect. And I would be grateful for that stain remover. Thank you."

"I bought this coffee downtown and it's actually pretty good."

"Anything would be better than what posed as coffee on the plane."

"I'm sure." She doesn't go into the kitchen, playing with the edge of a Band-Aid over her wrist. "When were you last here, in the Delta?"

"I believe it's been about eight or nine years."

"Does it seem like it's changed at all?"

He straightens. "Funny you mention it because thus far it seems remarkably *un*changed. I was thinking on the drive about how the *desire* to change is uniquely expressed in this landscape, by which I mean how the Mississippi River seeks to merge with the Atchafalaya River, which would of course flood this whole area, so that it would be a sort of Delta Atlantis, and how the Mississippi's desire to change course is thwarted by the Army Corp of Engineers. What's so fascinating to me is how the tension between our desire for stasis and the natural world's appetite for change is such a potent symbol for this region. Think about the way in which hurricanes, floods, extreme heat, and rich soil shape so much of the Global South. In a sense, the Delta is not supposed to be here."

Billie cocks her head a little to one side. "Huhn. I don't think I knew that about the Mississippi."

"There are some gorgeous maps charting how the course of the river has changed over the years." He could really do with that coffee. "Do you miss the city—Philadelphia I believe you said?"

"Yeah, Philly. Not really. I'll be back soon enough. It's weird but I don't even mind not having a dishwasher. You know, when I drive around here I get this title in my head, like if this place were a book it would be *Ruins: A Love Story*. But I thought that it was missing something, so maybe it's *Ruins: A Love Story; The Place That's Not Supposed to Be Here.*"

Before moving toward the kitchen, she smiles and Cliff James surfaces. An odd dissonance in his easy smile against her large, sad eyes. Although Melvin's book (tentatively entitled *Against Redemption: The Biography of Clifton James,* or, *The Prophet of Avalon: The Life of Clifton James*) centers primarily on the transformation of Cliff's work from deceptively simple almost Whitmanesque poetry to a pointed exploration of the contradictions of American blackness, Melvin is, of course, quite interested in Billie. Indeed, what she could tell him about her relationship with her father may shed much-needed light on what role fatherhood played in Cliff's life. And at the same time, Melvin has never been satisfied with his chapter on Cliff's return to Mississippi. What precisely was the rupture with the city? Of course, it was in one sense a homecoming, but in practical terms, it meant moving away from the hub of black literati in New York, where he was just starting to make inroads. The question isn't so much why did Cliff leave Harlem for Mississippi, but why at that particular moment?

Billie comes back in and hands him the stain stick. "I don't really have any food worth offering. Unless you're hungry for something very close to cheese?"

"I already ate. Thank you. Do you remember that there used to be another house right over there?" He points out of the front window.

"Harlan, Mr. McGee's son, said that it was my grandmother's house."

"Yes, and if I remember correctly, it was a smaller and of course much older structure. I wonder when it was torn down?"

"I think he said twenty years ago."

"This house"—he glances at a calendar of the Kennedys and MLK—"was built by your grandmother Ruby's family. Your grandfather, Willie, was in fact from the Hill country, but I'm sure you know all that." Even with the calendar, the room is monotonously stark. "I apologize if I'm being somewhat overbearing but it's helping me to retread this ground out loud."

"Not at all. Actually I don't know much about my grandfather. What was he like?"

He can't resist chewing a stick of gum, no matter how gauche it may be. "I think it would be fair to say that he was a hard man who lived a hard life. And like so many black veterans of World War II, he came back expecting to be treated with dignity and not as a second-class citizen. But instead he was greeted by this, I would say, surge of terror. What I mean is that many white men, particularly in the South, feared that these returning black veterans had forgotten their place. And consequently, you see a rise in lynchings. Even at the level of— I mean at the same time as this increase in violence, most black veterans are also being kept from receiving the benefits of the G.I. Bill, which in turn hinders the growth of a black middle class. No college, no housing loans, and so on. This is all to say that it seems to me a crucial mistake to write Willie, and men like him, off as wandering philanderers, and this is not to detract from the plight of single, black mothers, but to point out the complexities that—"

"My grandfather cheated on Grandma Ruby?"

"He left your grandmother. But that's a good example of where I would argue that while on one hand, yes clearly he had met another woman, but it was also very much about the effect of the daily humiliations he encountered on his return to Greendale, heightened by being treated quite differently in Europe. So I think that one of the particular questions he would have been facing was: How do I stay in an even more hostile, and in a number of ways potentially deadly, environment when I have risked my life for this country?"

The coffee machine beeps from the kitchen. Billie is staring at him. "You know so much more about my family than I do." It seems almost an accusation.

"I tend to run on when I'm excited. You must know I've been working on this—essentially portrait of your father—

for so many years. I may have said on the phone, but in this book I am, in a sense, trying to lay bare his creative process, his artistic transformation, and by degrees, his life. Which is all to say, although I have this glut of information, you know, it hardly equals the bond between you and your father."

Her eyes are on the dog, gently tapping the tip of her shoe against the bottom of one of his paws. "I'm not sure how much of a bond I can have. I mean, I don't remember much. You would think that because he died thirty years ago, it would get easier. But weirdly the older I get the more I feel the loss." She looks up at him. "Anyway. Cream? Sugar?"

"Both if you wouldn't mind."

She disappears into the kitchen. A spoon taps against the side of a mug. He sits on a rather ghastly brown armchair.

When she comes back, she seems soft with thought. "I never met my grandfather. But he was alive when my father died, right?"

"Yes." Perhaps it is wrong to drown her immediately in all of these narratives. What he's privy to—well, he has a certain distance as an observer, almost a kind of detective.

She hands him a purple mug. "Did he come to the funeral?"

"Yes." He reads the side of the mug—BLESSED.

She smiles. "I bought it at a garage sale. It seemed to fit the house. Did you go to the funeral?"

"Oh no, I had just started my master's and hadn't been introduced to your father's work yet. Actually one of my future professors was there. And what I find fascinating about the funeral is that though Cliff wasn't a member of the Harlem Writers Guild, and he appears to only have attended a single workshop held by Umbra, there were a not insubstantial number of black academics and writers in attendance. So you can see that he had been making connections in the literary community. I mean, the fact that his work had appeared in *Negro Digest, Leaves, Othering, Nkombo,* and the *Black Scholar* is considerable."

"My mother wasn't there, right?"

"I don't believe she was."

"Do you know why not?"

"I don't, though I do find it curious because she would have been in Greendale to retrieve you. You find it odd as well?"

Something to make note of. Cliff had a relatively stormy relationship with Pia, though how well Billie is familiar with the fights, occasional disappearances, and other women remains to be seen. And, of course, there was the strain of an interracial relationship at that time—the lack of places they could go together, the disapproval from Pia's family not to mention his own, and even from some colleagues and friends for *talking black but sleeping white* as they say.

"So where did my grandfather end up?"

"St. Louis. He lived with a woman there and they had a daughter together."

"My father had a half sister? So, technically I have an aunt. Well anyway, you came all this way for a reason." She drags a box across the remarkably bare room. "I found the manuscript in here. I've checked through all of these records at least three times, but I haven't found anything else. Then"—she drags another box over—"this one has some of my mother's letters and notes on her second book. She didn't have time to finish it. It could have something relevant in it." Billie takes a stack of papers that are sitting on a striped folding chair. "And this is it, the chapter."

"Let me wash my hands." He goes into the kitchen and runs the hot water, scrubbing then drying his hands thoroughly with what he hopes is a clean dish towel. He picks up the papers, the original documents with—wait—handwriting around the typed words. Clifton James marginalia! Extraordinary. There could be, should be something like a two-day symposium featuring the documents. After the biography goes to press, of course.

He takes a scarf from his briefcase. "It's clean." He rolls it out on the living room floor, then separates the papers along it. "I'll photograph each. I've brought some polyester sleeves and I have an acid-free box in the car." He looks at her. "If you don't mind?"

She's frowning. "Of course. But don't you want to read it first?"

"I'm dying to read it. But I am also deeply aware of what a marvelous find this is and I must preserve it just in case." Just in case it spontaneously combusts. He takes out his camera and snaps the photographs. The dog opens its eyes to check on his movements, then yawns, rolling onto its other side.

As he's taking the last photo, she says, "Doesn't Rufus look two dimensional? Like a fourteenth-century hound. My mom used to have pictures of this illuminated manuscript she was obsessed with, *Le Livre de la Chasse*. It means slaying the boar—you probably know that already."

"Oh no, my French is quite rusty." He lowers the camera. It's true. The dog's front and back paws are perfectly stacked.

"We lived there for a few months, Paris. But I was only three, so I don't really remember."

"Was the book a kind of medieval hunting guide?"

"Yeah, for noblemen, of course. It had all of these elaborate rules and rituals of the hunt."

He puts away the camera. "Do you write?"

She laughs. "Grant proposals. You know, now that I think of it, my mom was going to take me to the Morgan Library in New York to see the manuscript. But she got too sick. After she died, I thought about flying out to L.A. to the Getty and seeing it there. It was winter in Philly and so depressing, you know? I kept picturing myself sitting out in the sun by a pool for hours and going to the Getty. But I never did." She reaches down to pet the dog. "He killed his son."

"Pardon?"

"The guy who wrote *Le Livre de la Chasse*. Count Gaston. Or Jean. Pierre?"

Better get close-ups of the marginalia. He takes the camera back out.

She sits sideways on the armchair, her legs flopped over one arm. "So what do you think publishing his biography will do after all this time?"

"My hope is that others discover him and that his work is placed among the other great black American writers."

"Have you heard of Mae Cowdery?"

"Yes, of course, though I admit it's been years since I've read her."

He waits for her to go on, but Billie gets up and floats back into the kitchen. Such a lovely girl, woman. There is an element . . . the term is *arrested*. He puts away the camera again and takes out his notepad. It is possible that her childhood was, in a sense, arrested. Perhaps a part of her lingers there on that porch—this porch—waiting for her father. She was in the house asleep. Though Billie's time line on the night Cliff died is something that's also never entirely been clear to him. But he won't bring up such a delicate matter yet. Oh boy, he's drinking much too much coffee. It's giving him the jitters. He can't drink this much if he isn't smoking. Why is quitting so damn oppressive? Where is the joy at the new expansion in his lungs? Concentrate, man, concentrate. This is one of the greatest days of your life! He sits down cross-legged on the floor, exposing his ankles, and reads. What he wouldn't give for a cigarette. What strikes him most as he reads is that if in "Chapter 2" Cliff is already discussing his time as a Freedom Rider, then the book must have been neither a traditional memoir nor a coming-of-age memoir, which would have started at his childhood and probably reached his civil rights awakening in the second half. The book must center around something else.

With care, he opens the second box, lifting out a brown paper bag. Inside are three tiny teeth wrapped in cotton wool, a hint of brown at their roots.

"Oh god, those are mine," says Billie as she steps back in. "Is it strange to keep your child's teeth?"

"I don't have children."

"My mother liked bones."

He laughs with her. This may be the— There is a way of

asking gently, of course, with sensitivity. "I'm not sure yet if I will be able to stay much past the weekend, so although I hesitate to ask—"

"What is it?" she says, her forehead tensing.

"As I explore the limits of what this biography can be, first and foremost a reflection on a certain historical moment, a deconstruction of Cliff's work, the way he plays with formal structures, and I hope a thorough examination of his position in the context of the Civil Rights Movement and the Black Arts Movement and the tensions therein, simultaneously there's a mystery at the heart of the book."

"Okay?" A hand goes to her pursed lips.

"With regard to the circumstances of his death. I mean, in no way do I want your father's work to be obscured by those circumstances, but nor can I ignore that they exist."

Billie nods slowly. "Of course not."

"But in order to do justice to that mystery, I do need access to certain documents. In particular, the police report."

She looks troubled. Their pleasant tête-à-tête disrupted. Could he have not waited until they'd known each other more than an hour?

"Isn't it public record?"

"In this county, it's at the discretion of the department. In this case, the report is only available to family members. And since it wasn't something that went to trial, there aren't court records."

She stares at the floor, moving a socked toe back and forth over a rut in the wood. "I guess so. I mean, you know what you need to really tell his story. And I'd be curious to know what it says. Maybe it mentions me. I didn't tell you but I met Jerry Hopsen the other day. Have you heard of him?"

"Oh yes, a childhood friend of your father's. He's in my mental database."

"Right. And he said something about my picture coming on the news after my father died because I'd gone missing. Have you heard anything about that?"

"No, never." He picks his notepad up off the floor. "That's incredible. It's never come up. I can't recall seeing it in any news reports."

"I think it came on the local news, maybe only for a few hours."

"What did Mr. Hopsen say exactly? This is quite something."

"That I was missing and my grandmother put my picture on the news. But then my uncle says that the police couldn't find me and freaked my grandmother out and that I was only missing for a couple of hours. But that's not the way Mr. Hopsen made it sound."

"It could be that one of them misremembers. People's memories tend to refashion themselves around a particular narrative over time."

"Sure, but I'd like to know what actually happened. Maybe the police report would help me do that?"

"It's possible, but in any case I do think that it is absolutely invaluable to the biography." He sips his coffee. It's already cold. He puts the mug down and reaches into his briefcase for a gift bag. "A small token of my appreciation."

"Oh, you didn't need to get me anything." She takes the bag and pulls out a pint of bourbon. "Wow."

"I haven't had this particular brand, but it comes highly recommended."

"Thanks." She slips the bottle back in.

"Can I ask who else knows about the chapter?"

"Just you and my cousin Lola. I mean, other people might know it exists, but you guys are the only ones I've told."

"I know you are waiting on divulging this to your uncle, but would you consider not telling anyone else for the time being? Only because there are a couple of scholars who would whip out a few trivial essays on it and undermine the publication of the book."

"Are there other Cliff James scholars? You're the only one I've heard of."

"There are other scholars interested in him, though I'm not certain they would say that they specialize in his work."

She runs her thumb back and forth along the side of the gift bag. "Do you think my father had an accident? Or maybe that it was something else?"

There is a very intense look on her face. The space between them has edges. Best to proceed very carefully here. "If you mean foul play, while it's not improbable that the local police during that time could have been involved in the death of a black man, my question would be why Clifton James? And why in 1972 and not years before when he was an activist? I've never uncovered that he was in any sort of dispute. If he was a victim of circumstance it seems odd that it would occur at his house, on his property with nothing stolen, et cetera. Well actually, his girlfriend at the time did make the suggestion of— She did suspect foul play, but she didn't seem to have any sense of who or why, and it seems

possible that it was just grief talking. My experience studying racially motivated killings has been that though one person may have pulled the trigger so to speak, there's a way in
which it is almost always a communal effort, and there's no
evidence of that here."

"I was actually thinking suicide. But you're saying like
a mob?"

"Let's think about Emmett Till. In the most popular
narrative, he was murdered by two white men, Milam and
Bryant. But there were many more people present, moving
the body, cleaning up the evidence, participating—you see,
a communal effort. I've actually been hearing rumors that
the FBI might reopen that case. But I don't think we should
jump to any conclusions about your father without evidence."

There's a loose piece of paper from the box with two lines
scrawled in pen. *You have here no lasting home. You are a
stranger and a pilgrim wherever you may be, and you shall have
no rest . . .* "What is this?" He hands it to Billie.

Her eyes run along the lines. "Oh, it's Thomas à Kempis.
A German monk. He wrote a book that was important to
my mom. I don't remember what it was called." She becomes
quite still then looks up. "Good, isn't it?"

She lets the dog out and goes onto the porch. Melvin
follows, holding the chapter. They watch the dog chase birds
fruitlessly across the yard.

"You can read it in peace inside. I'll stay out here with
the dog. Shit." Billie hops off the porch as the dog bounds
into the road. "Rufus, come!"

The dog scampers over the road and into the field on the
other side. Melvin goes down the steps.

"Rufus! Come!" She turns back to Melvin. "God, he's never gone so far. He's a speck already."

"I'm sure he'll come back. For food if nothing else."

"Yeah, well, I don't want to lose my dog to the Delta. Wait here. It's muddy." Billie sprints across the road and into the turnrows, hunting her noble hound.

BILLIE

THE GREENDALE POLICE STATION IS A SQUAT BRICK BUILDING LOW
ceilinged and fluorescent lit. Billie parks next to a battered
red pickup truck with a BUSH/CHENEY bumper sticker and
a rifle locked on a rack. Cracking the windows, she leaves
Rufus on the backseat with a rawhide treat, which he does
not appreciate, yipping and scratching. If only she could
bring him.

Before the doors, she spits out her gum. To appear professional. Like someone who has done this before and could
do it again. Someone who will not burst into hysterics when
the file touches her hands. Or run screaming down the road
after she reads it.

After passing through heavy glass doors and the arch
of a metal detector, there is a resigned black woman with
bobbed hair behind the counter who without looking at her
while she talks says that it'll be a minute. Billie goes to let

Rufus out. He jumps from the car and itches his neck with his hind leg. Together, they tour the sad yellow parking lot grass overlaying the medians.

Back in the station lobby, an officer comes out and asks her to step into the hallway from which he's just emerged. The hall door shuts behind her with a sucking sound.

"Ms. James, I'm Sheriff Oakes." He smiles, resting in his bulk like an armchair.

She shakes his offered hand. "Hello." She was expecting someone to hand her a file and that would be it. But it's a small town, so maybe this is how it goes.

"I wanted to come on out here, Ms. James, and introduce myself. My father was one of the officers who worked the case back in '72 as the responding. He passed a couple years ago, otherwise I know he would have spoken to you himself."

The sheriff has thickly chapped lips that she finds distracting. "I'm sorry to hear that." She looks away from his mouth. "Thanks for meeting with me."

"Let's head on over to my office."

As they turn the cinder block corner, they enter a carpeted space, a few officers hunched in cubicles glancing at her from under anemic lighting.

The sheriff stops at a desk where a middle-aged secretary with stiff blond hair sits on the phone. Her watery blue eyes meet his. "Janice can get you a coffee or water. When she's done with whatever she's doing, that is."

"That's okay, thanks. I don't have long," Billie says, wishing she were back in the car with Rufus.

He walks into his office and she follows, leaving the door cracked. One can only hope to count on Janice if things get weird.

The walls of his office are lined with awards, newspaper clippings, photographs of him with state representatives, of him fishing with small children, and a large crucifix. The only window looks out onto a back parking lot. He sits down behind his desk, moving his coffee cup from a folder.

He points at the water stains on the low ceiling. "They haven't remodeled this place in thirty years. There's faulty vents up there. Likely asbestos too."

She sits in the hard chair in front of his desk. "Mind if I ask why I'm back here? I was under the impression I was just picking something up."

"I wanted to be up front with you about the case. I swear it's always bothered me."

"Could you elaborate?"

"It seems to me like they ain't had a whole lot to go on back then. Part of that is they didn't have the technology we do now, if you know what I mean." He takes a handkerchief from his pocket and wipes his hairline. "Always so dang hot in here this time of day."

Her teeth are almost chattering with cold.

"Now, I don't know what you've been told, but it's my job to make sure you have all the facts." He continues in a slightly more formal tone. "In the report, and again not sure what your family may have told you, but they ruled your father's death an accident." The AC clicks on, stale cold air rushing down the vents overhead, making the cobwebs in the corner of the ceiling flutter. "Finally." He puts the handkerchief down. "I know that my daddy explored all the angles. I remember that."

"But how would you remember?"

"When I was about eighteen, I worked here in a part-time capacity for my daddy. He was the deputy sheriff then." He pauses to sip his coffee. "I remember them looking at a couple of potential suspects. But it was all conjecture."

"Who did they look at?"

"First, at your mother. But now that's standard procedure, most homicides being done by the spouse. She had a solid alibi in Philadelphia."

Nausea pushes through her stomach. "Did they think it looked suspicious?"

"Just being thorough." He sets down his coffee. "Then they looked at your uncle."

"My uncle?"

"Thing was, he owed your father some money. This being a small town, people knew how he'd been gambling, going beyond his means."

"But he was young. I mean, my father barely had any money, so it can't have been much."

"I guess not enough to support his being a suspect. Personally, I knew Dee wasn't involved in that way. What they did find for certain is that your father had a high blood alcohol content at the time of his death. And I've seen this kind of thing happen on the job countless times with hard drinkers. And this is just my honest-to-god personal opinion, but I believe that rather than it being accidental, he was trying to take his own life." He lays his hands on the folder on the desk. "See I say this because it's real common that when the notion of suicide enters the picture, a family can't imagine their loved one taking their own life and so they often want it to be something else, anything else, even foul play."

He is waiting for her to respond. Finally she says, "I guess it could have been suicide, but it was a fall, so I don't see how that works. And I find the idea of my uncle hurting my father ridiculous." Her throat is tight. "I just want the report and to read it for myself. Can I do that please?"

"Of course." He picks up the folder under his hands. "I just wanted to share with you what I knew."

But it's not what he knows, it's what he thinks. She stuffs the folder in her purse and stands.

"I apologize for not being of more use. I wish my father was still around to give you the particulars."

"Great, thanks." She takes one last look at him in his congratulatory office. "You've seen a lot, being a sheriff."

He stands as well. "Sure have."

"What happens to all that?"

"All what?"

"All you've seen."

"It's right here." He taps the side of his head.

"It must be hard," she says. "So many bad things." She goes to the door.

"You in town for long?"

She stops, turns. "No."

"Well, you let me know if you have any questions. I'd be happy to try to answer them for you." He digs in his desk drawer and holds out a card. "Let me give you this in case you think of anything."

"I won't need it," she says and is out the door.

IN THE CAR, SHE TEARS OPEN THE REPORT AS IF SHE WILL NOT LIVE long enough to see it, but the details don't make much of a narrative. Bruises on his face, penetrating wounds on his arms—could have been caused by a fall. Contusions, abrasions on head and face, upper and lower extremities, blood spatter on the ground—the subdural hematoma that killed him. Cause of death ruled blunt force trauma. Found in the yard. No signs in the house of a struggle or forced entry or burglary. No witnesses. Front door left ajar. His brother concerned of his whereabouts, he came by the house and found him. Nine one one was called. Ruby James identified the body of her son. Ruled an accident, multiple falls while intoxicated.

She can't remember the first time that she was told of her father's death, can't picture the exact day. Or remember when it was that she later thought to ask exactly how he died and her mother told her an accident, a misadventure she said. Not suicide. Not Uncle Dee. Nothing but a tragic freak accident, which can happen, does happen, and happened to Daddy.

She turns the AC up full blast and bends her face to the vent. The sweet synthetic funk of her deodorant fills the car. She digs through her bag to find her phone. The call to her uncle goes straight to voice mail. She could call Jude but instead she reads the report again. Deputy Oakes, that's Sheriff Oakes's father. Deputy Roberts, no idea. Deputy

McGee. How did she miss that? McGee. She presses the heels of her palms to her eyes. Everywhere her family was, the McGees were too. Goddamn it, Mississippi.

On the drive back, she racks her brain for actual experiences of her father. Not stories about him, or things that he wrote—just her with him. There's a day they were rushing through a market as it started to rain and everyone was hurrying to pack up and cover their wares. Her hand was in his and he was pulling her along. Fat raindrops on the plastic over racks of clothes. They were laughing.

Then one time he was lifting her onto his mother's bed. Grandmomma Ruby sitting up to hold her with hands exquisitely dark and bone thin. She was sick with something and Billie was a little scared but didn't want to act scared in front of him. Soon she didn't mind the smiling, sunken face of the old woman. Then the door closed and they were alone in the darkened room muffled by heat and curtains. Because he left. Without saying where he was going. But he would be back. She knew that. Just not when.

Her mother wrote a paper about parenthood in the fourteenth century that examined the high mortality rate of children and then the apprentice system, where rich kids were sent to serve and live in another house at a young age. At the time of its publication, some believed that medieval parents were inured to the frequent death of their children, indifferent to them out of necessity. But her mother argued that it wasn't that they didn't feel deep grief or love, but that they cultivated a kind of compassionate detachment toward their small children, since they couldn't control what might easily befall them. That and they believed that they would be reunited. If Billie could believe that she would be reunited with her parents, she could forgive her life for everything.

She walks with Rufus through the woods. The wind is high and the trees shift and groan as if getting comfortable. They take a different path to the creek, this one softly plowed through the mud. On the bank is a white church steeple sitting on the grass as if the body of the church is growing underground. At the top of the steeple is a broken cross. It looks like a forlorn vestige of a world that is an exact replica of theirs but now a level below. As if every few thousand years, the earth buries itself and remakes everyone all over again, and they arrive bringing the same chaos, the same longing, the same blind, inevitable end.

She sits, temporarily unafraid of snakes—the black racers or ribbon snakes, speckled kings or cottonmouths. Or is she welcoming a bite in this bloom of old grief? Her uncle says do not try and suck the poison, do not get a knife to cut it out. If she stepped into that milky red water, it would keep her from seeing or hearing, it would swallow her up, it would be the warm earth all around, pulsing lazily against her aching head.

Rufus knocks into her leg. She strokes his nose as he lies down next to her on the bank. The sparse wet grass is seeping into her pants. Above them the sky is made of bright gray light.

Back at the house, she paces the living room with a bottle of whiskey. The calls to her uncle have gone unanswered. Rufus lies on the floor by the screen door, his eyes half open, paws going as he dreams. Outside, thunder claps so hard that it shakes the floor, suspended as it is only a few feet from the ground. Rufus opens his bleary eyes, locates her, and closes them again.

On the porch in the warm spatter of rain, Billie feels perilously sober. No witnesses the report said. So where was she that night? When she goes back in, she wraps herself in her sleeping bag and walks into the closet, shutting the door. She sits and closes her eyes. There would be the darkness of her narrow room, flickering colored light over the kitchen from the TV in the living room. The laughter track bursting between the clicking of the rotating fan. The front door opens and closes, opens and slams. Feet. The clatter of something falling to the floor that does not break. If someone looks in, she mustn't move. Not be seen or heard. Eyes closed or something bad.

DR. MELVIN HURLEY

HE IS SURPRISED TO LEAVE HIS MOTEL AND STUMBLE UPON A RE-
markably well-curated bookstore among the vacant buildings downtown. As he holds the door, a series of coiffed older
white women shuffle past him in their precariously stacked
heels. Under their smiles, he senses a smidgeon of confusion
as he goes in, walking toward the photo books through their
unrelenting perfume.

He will of course be told that he is not from around
here. It happens multiple times whenever he visits. Embedded in this phrase is not so much a reference to his accent or
his (cosmopolitan) wit, but to his unexpected lack of defer-
ence. The way in which his posture does not ask if his body
is allowed to take up its space. Or sometimes, in more casual
interactions, they'll say *You don't see color*. The utter irony of
this has always struck him, as he told his partner last night
on the phone. On a certain level it seems like the only way

they can explain him is to imagine he is safe from being reminded at any moment of the weight of his color—*little peltings* he calls them—like being hit with rotten eggs when he didn't even know he was onstage. Even now, even now in his early fifties, these small displays of hostility have the ability to take him by surprise. He still finds himself asking if it is really happening. Did that flight attendant really ignore him? Did that white woman really clutch her purse and cross the street? Did that cabbie really stop and take one look at him then drive away?

All that aside, it is a gloriously sunny morning in the Delta where the air has the sense of being washed clean and he is standing in the Southern Writers section holding a lightly used copy of Cliff's last book of poetry, *Flatbottom Unrest*. If he expected to unearth anything at all, it would have been Cliff's first book, *Race Records,* which is much more accessible, more of a fluid meditation on the contradictory spell of the South.

When Cliff's biography comes out—he has just had a wonderful conversation with his editor this morning—there should be a reissuing of Cliff's poetry with the new introduction to *Flatbottom* that he started working on in the shower. Something along the lines of . . . a mythic refutation of the conventional, a reclamation of Blackness, by which he would be gesturing toward the phrases in Arabic, its psychedelic odes, references to Boccaccio, Jean Toomer, C. L. R. James, etc. But the author photo must remain the same: Cliff, unsmiling in a black beret.

Melvin flips to the poem "Story 1937."

the leather strap   the broom   the switch
habits before freedom
freedom: the lie which is true
before: kept fed but close to death

the penitentiary   the gun   the rope
is at hand now that you free
free: kept down with your eyes down
now: night riders patrol in cars

those born again   die free
a lie for grateful slaves
grateful: who are better off
lie: who is better off

dig down into the unmarked earth
lay there and be free

Perhaps in the introduction he should note that it wasn't
until his first year in his Ph.D. program that he encountered
Clifton James, a footnote in an essay in a Black Arts anthology. The footnote offered a truly fascinating description of
Cliff's poetry as provocatively moving—from collective dia-
sporic dirges to the simply vivid poems of the dispossessed.
But no one Melvin knew seemed to have a copy of Cliff's
work. The university library listed a copy of *Race Records*
(1967) as available, but it was not in the prescribed spot.
One of his professors had let an old student borrow his copy
of *Flatbottom Unrest* (1969) but couldn't remember who the

student was, or even what year they had graduated. The small press that had published scant copies of both books had been shuttered in 1972, which was the year that Cliff died. But rather than signal the end of his search, the detective story became something of a quest.

He was rewarded almost a year later, when at a conference, a speaker quoted from one of Cliff's poems. The poem, unknown to Melvin at the time, had this profoundly tribal intimacy. The invaluable speaker turned out to be an old friend of Cliff's. It was this crucial happenstance that culminated in a first edition of each book and even an old copy of a 1969 literary magazine called *Shadowplay*.

Not that he would include this part, but it wasn't until Melvin's paper on Cliff had met with a certain level of success that he truly began thinking of writing a biography. By then his friends were joking that as the only Clifford James scholar he should be called the (Other) Jamesian. But he wasn't emboldened enough to undertake it until his first book on Langston Hughes and George Schuyler was under contract. Buoyed by this, he contacted Cliff's brother and made his first visit to the Delta. At the time, Dee James had just been made Cliff's literary executor. To begin with, Dee seemed grateful that his brother's work was getting serious critical attention, but when Melvin brought up the biography, Dee became distant, even when Melvin assured him that though it would follow the narrative of Cliff's life, revealing his way of looking at the world, at its deepest root it would be a scholarly work and give Cliff's poetry the attention it deserved. But once Melvin left the Delta, Dee stopped taking his calls. Nevertheless, Melvin forged ahead, finding artists who had known Cliff, even a couple of distant family members willing to talk. Getting in touch with Pia proved elusive until she joined a university faculty in the mid-eighties. But in her, he found his staunchest opponent. Cliff would never want that, she said. For the public to read about his failures, his affairs, his sad, useless death. He would never want Billie to read about that. But it turns out she was wrong about Billie.

On one hand, it is true that any number of artists' biographies feature bereft children, haunted widows, bitterly fractured families left behind by the alcoholic poet, or the hermit poet, Gilded Age poet, fractured war poet, the poet with other families, other lives. But to place Clifton James within his historical context, a black poet so prolific during his short life and amid such a turbulent time, is to understand what he had left to write, and somehow, Melvin suspects, why he died at that particular moment. Over the years, he has been inclined to think it more likely than not that Cliff's death was probably an accident. But for him this has never meant that there were not forces conspiring to bring it about. Think of the return to the uneasy tension of a partially desegregated rural Mississippi, the agitated marriage to a white woman and subsequent divorce, the separation from his young child, the moving home to care for his elderly mother, add alcohol and that *something else* which persists. In essence, it is hardly an exaggeration to say that the life of Melvin Hurley has been haunted by the life of Clifton James.

Melvin doesn't buy the book. By now he has countless copies not to mention every literary journal that ever featured or mentioned Cliff, and besides the toothpicks, his briefcase is full with Robin D. G. Kelley's *Freedom Dreams: The Black Radical Imagination; Robert Hayden: Essays on the Poetry* edited by Laurence Goldstein and Robert Chrisman; and a copy of the spring edition of the *African American Review.* He actually has a book review coming out in September in their summer/fall "Amiri Baraka" issue.

On the drive to meet Billie, Melvin admires the serene expanse of the fields, their verdure, though even at that moment his pleasure is problematized by his imagining the long ten-foot cotton sacks black folk dragged through the turn-rows, working from can to can't.

When he pulls into what functions as a driveway, Billie is sitting on the edge of the porch, swinging one foot, in a kind of roller derby ensemble: T-shirt, ripped denim shorts, and striped socks. A file folder sits between her and the dog who leaps off the porch as Melvin steps from the car, bounding ominously toward him.

"Rufus," she says.

The dog slows, sniffing his leg. Melvin tries to pat its head, but it's moving too much.

"You remember him, Rufus." She snaps her fingers, then stands and slaps her leg. The dog returns to her side.

"More obedient today," he says, walking up the porch steps.

"I've been working on his manners." She looks down at the file. "Well, there it is." Her voice is a little hoarse. "I've read it a few times. I think . . . I'll let you be the judge." She picks up the file and hands it to him. "I'll tell you about the bizarre time I had at the station when you're done reading." There's a certain kind of brittle languor about her today.

"Thank you for getting this. I realize that it must have been an especially difficult task for you. But I do think it's incredibly important for us to have it. And when I use the term *difficult,* I am deeply aware of how insufficient it is in this case."

"Yeah." She pushes a wisp of hair behind her ear. "It just makes me feel tired. I was thinking last night of him all alone out there in trouble." She looks at the front yard then into the woods. "He could have collapsed anywhere out here. I guess I knew that. And there's—" Her eyes are shiny. "He lost a tooth. It got knocked out somehow."

"Are you still comfortable staying here?"

"I wouldn't exactly say comfortable." She yanks a string off of the edge of her shorts. "I feel like it's where I need to be. I'll leave you to it." She goes inside.

To a certain degree, very little in the file is a surprise. Except for one thing that poses a considerable number of new questions.

Inside, Billie is sitting on a dirty sleeping bag on the floor, her knees curled to her chest, an unopened book by her side. She looks up. "That was fast."

"Let me begin with this: I would say that I know something of the complex relationship between your family and the McGees. And there's a long tradition of these kind of quasi-familial bonds in the Delta between plantation owners and their black sharecroppers. That being said, there's nothing cut-and-dry about these relationships, they're tremendously fluid. I mean, what has always fascinated me is that while there may be love and care exchanged, the white family would never typically socialize with the black family, not past the age of twelve or thirteen. You wouldn't see them having each other over for dinner or going to the movies together. And this is what I get the sense was the case with your father and Mr. McGee. In his own fashion, Mr. McGee confirmed this with me when I interviewed him in the early nineties. But what makes me—I don't think it's an exaggeration to say what shocks me—is that at no time did he mention that he was one of the officers who found your father's body."

She gets to her knees, sitting back on her heels. "But not only that. My uncle never said anything about it. Honestly, I might not even think it was that big of a deal if people didn't keep leaving it out."

"Though this particular officer may not be our Mr. McGee. It could be that it's a relative, a cousin perhaps."

"It could be but I bet it wasn't." She chews her bottom lip. "You know, my uncle told me to go to Mr. McGee if I needed any help. He said Mr. McGee knew our family. That seems so cryptic now."

He sets down his briefcase. "And then there is the fact that your grandmother bought this piece of land from them, which was quite unusual for the time. Many farmers in the Delta have sold land to large agricultural companies, but very rarely to former black tenants."

"Do they not sell to old tenants because the tenants don't have the money, or something else?"

He drags the deck chair closer to her and sits. "I imagine that the two aren't unrelated. I get the sense that black people don't own much if anything in the Delta. I mean, of course they have gained some political footing since the Movement, but the upper echelon of the white population has mostly kept what money there is."

"My uncle must know."

"Do you think he would consider talking to me? We haven't spoken in years. It turned out that he wasn't comfortable with the idea of Cliff having a biography."

"Maybe it's better if I talk to him first. If he ever calls me back. I won't mention that you're here yet." Billie is quiet for a moment, rubbing her fingers over the knuckles of her opposite hand.

He leans forward to wipe the dust from his loafer. "You mentioned a strange interaction at the police station?"

"Yeah, get this—the sheriff, who is the fucking son of the Oakes in the report, told me that he thought my father committed suicide. Why would he pull me aside to say that? So bizarre." She moves to sit with her back against the wall. "I thought I was picking up the report from the front desk, but he came to get me and brought me to his office."

"Although southerners do pride themselves on their friendliness, that does seem a bit unusual." Melvin takes out a notepad.

"His excuse was that he was working at the department when it happened. Then he implied my father was an alcoholic." She looks up at him. "You don't think there's any truth to that, do you?"

"That's not the sense I've gotten. In that period of his

life, I would say, I would call him a hard drinker rather than an alcoholic. I think it's important that we talk to Mr. Mc-Gee. Let's—"

"I know. But not yet. I need to talk to my uncle first."

"Okay, let me make a copy of the report and at least make an appointment with Mr. McGee. In the meantime, why don't you get out of the house for a while and do something utterly unrelated?"

"I guess that would be the healthy thing." She stands, bending to roll up the sleeping bag. "But really, is there anything in this whole town that doesn't touch it in some way?"

BILLIE

THERE ARE HIGH HEELS IN HER SUITCASE. AS IF SHE EVER WEARS them in Philly let alone out here in the Delta where she knows next to nobody. Her mother rarely wore makeup. Pia was compact, unapologetic. She walked and biked, wasn't one to show a lot of skin. Angry when someone was surprised that Billie was her daughter. The double take at Pia's blond hair, the long, slightly openmouthed stare at Billie's skin: the *You're her mother?* But Billie always knew they looked alike.

There is a knock at the door. Rufus looks over to where she sits on the mattress, still picking at one last nugget of possibly infected gravel in her hand. He trots into the living room, barking. Through the bedroom window she sees her uncle.

She runs to the door and, holding Rufus back by the collar, opens it. "Where have you been? I must've called you a hundred times—why haven't you called me back? Rufus, hush." She lets go of him so that he can sniff her uncle.

"That's why I come by." Her uncle looks like he has just woken up or never been to sleep.

"I got the police report," she says.

He stares at her. "Why you do that? Why you want to go opening up old wounds?"

"I wanted to know what happened."

He leans his shoulder against the screen door. "Nobody know what happened. It wasn't ever investigated right. To the police it was just another black man who's dead."

"And so Mr. McGee, Jim McGee, was he one of the officers?"

A sigh passes through him. "He didn't find my brother, but he was one of the ones there."

"Why didn't you tell me that?"

"Ain't unusual. Greendale is a small town. We all wrapped up in each other's business. I knew the undertaker too. The way I see it, I ain't know what happened now or then. But I'm at peace with it." With his red eyes and drawn face, he doesn't look like somebody at peace.

"What did Grandmomma Ruby think?"

"That she didn't want more trouble." He turns and walks down the porch. She steps out and pushes Rufus back in. The birds are shouting, ignoring the impending rain.

"But it was her son," says Billie. "Didn't she want to make sure it was an accident?"

Her uncle lights a cigarette. "You have to understand that back then you couldn't look whites in the eye, couldn't go through the front door, had to say yes Sir, yes Ma'am, and they call you boy no matter how old you were. When you pay for something at their store you had to put your money on the counter so your skin didn't touch theirs. Anything could be done to you for looking at a white man in the wrong way. Anything. She seen it done to folks she knew. There's no use being angry at her. You don't know what it was to live your days like that."

"But this happened in 1972."

He throws his hands up. "Greendale was segregated all the way up till '72! Till then there was nowhere in this town for a black person to eat."

She ties back her hair. "It's starting to rain. Let's go in."

"The porch got carpenter ants." He points at large black ants marching down the front step.

"Is that bad?"

"I'll mix you up some sugar water and boric acid, show you how to kill them."

"Okay. Want to come in?"

"We ain't got time for that. I come to take you to the bar."

"What bar? I don't have deodorant on."

"Place I frequent on the east side. Somebody want to meet you."

"Who?" she asks.

"You see," he says.

ON THEIR WAY TO THE BAR, THEY PASS THROUGH THE MONEYED SECtion of town lined with stately oaks defending the sidewalks from the scorch of the sun. There is a surfeit of white porches, white joggers, and American flags. When they cross the train tracks, it is as if a bomb made out of soda cans, glass, and plastic wrappers has gone off, making the houses askew and the sidewalks buckle. There are no white people here except a man staggering ghoulishly down the middle of the street, his limp brown hair tucked into the collar of his plaid shirt. He is overdressed for the heat and wearing Coke-bottle glasses, a stray cast member from an eighties made-for-TV movie where he played the pedophile in a white van. He does not seem to see their car at first, or anything really. But finally he sees the bumper, then her with a blank delight like she is the leader of his cult. They swerve, missing him by inches.

The bar is made of baby-blue cinder blocks and sits next to a bail bonds/beauty salon/bridal boutique. The bar is oddly ventilated; it doesn't have central air or windows, but a series of fans and units that keep it synthetically cool. Neo-soul plays softly under conversations coming from patrons that Billie can't see. Her uncle leads her to the back of the room where a massive but sleekly leonine woman sits against the wall so that she faces the entrance, surveying everyone who comes in. Her large black earrings match the black pattern of her white silk shirt, exposing the tips of her shoulders and the tops of her breasts. The woman isn't talking, her thumb and pointer finger wrapped around a dainty plastic cup. A man sits at her table wearing a red button-down shirt and diamond-studded cross, his attention moving back and forth between his phone and the bottle of orange-flavored vodka at the center of the table.

Her uncle stops before the woman's chair. "This is Billie."

"Hi," Billie says.

The woman doesn't meet her eyes. "Sit down and pull up a chair, but don't bump the table and knock over the drinks because then it's over." She is speaking to Billie but looking at her uncle, as if holding him responsible for her behavior.

"Billie, this is Carlotta." Her uncle sets her a chair at the table.

Billie sits, not sure if she is supposed to know who that is.

"Why don't you make yourself useful and get the girl something to drink," Carlotta says.

Billie pulls a twenty from her back pocket. "I'll have whatever you're having."

"It's been a long time," Carlotta says.

"Has it? I'm sorry, but I don't think I know who you are." She looks up at her uncle.

"Carlotta was your daddy's girlfriend," he says.

Sometimes there were women at her father's. No one whose name she remembers. All she remembers is that she didn't like them.

"I told you she was too young," her uncle says.

"My father had a lot of girlfriends," she says.

Carlotta's eyes flicker to her. Yes, touché.

Carlotta lifts up her cup, sipping slowly. "Dee tells me you been asking questions about your daddy's death."

Her uncle is still hovering. Her mother had a print of the Röttgen Pietà, a fourteenth-century German sculpture. In it, a mutilated Christ lies emaciated in Mary's lap, ribs showing, mouth fallen open, tiny compared to the mass of his mother. But it is Mary's stony expression that is so disturbing: the wooden, embittered agony.

"She got the police report," her uncle says.

They all look at him, even the man in red stops texting.

"Why didn't you tell me that?" Carlotta says.

He is looking down. "I ain't know nothing about it till now."

Carlotta sucks her teeth. "You shouldn't have let her do that."

"I said I didn't know about it."

"You still messing with that white girl?"

Her uncle rolls his eyes to the ceiling. The man in red chuckles.

"You ain't ever learn. Go on and get her a drink. What you waiting for?"

He shakes his head but walks toward the bar.

Carlotta looks at Billie. "So now they know you digging around. I don't know what they like in Philadelphia, but out here we got uncles whose bodies we still can't find." She puts the cup down, gesturing to the man in red. "This is my partner, Donut." Donut nods without looking up from his phone. "We have an interior design company. Just got new business cards made." There's a stack next to her hand and she slides one toward Billie.

"It's a good logo." Billie makes a show of inspecting it. "What's wrong with getting the report? It seems pretty logical to me if I want to know what happened."

"But who wrote that report?" Carlotta holds her cup out to Donut, who tops it off. "And you're advertising to them that you're investigating."

"I'm not investigating. I'm a grant writer."

"What you call it then?"

"I'm finding out. As is my right."

Carlotta waves this aside. "Listen, before you do any more finding out, I need you to agree that you won't bring no trouble on Dee."

They both look at her uncle as he reaches across the bar for two little cups of liquor. "I wouldn't. What do you mean?"

"He's a bad luck man as it is. I know Miss Ruby wouldn't want him to suffer more than he has already." Carlotta adjusts her neckline. "The police ain't gonna help you none. Far as they concerned, it's over and done with and they won't like you not coming to that same conclusion. And men like Sheriff Oakes? The truth ain't in them."

"I know they didn't do a thorough investigation. Maybe they didn't care what happened, or maybe they just didn't know. But I won't be bothering them beyond getting the report." Her uncle has been stopped by a woman going up to the bar. "Do you think it's possible that my father could've committed suicide?"

"Never. He knew he was put on this earth for a reason."

"So what do you think happened?"

"Baby, somebody killed him."

Billie sits back. The music is squeezing the sides of her head.

"Always thought it, always will," Carlotta says.

She knew this was coming. That someone would say it. She didn't think it would come like this, but then she didn't know Carlotta existed.

"Do you remember anything?" Carlotta says.

"No." But now she can see him falling, his head dented open, grass rising all around him.

"But when I said it, didn't you feel I was right?"

"I don't know."

"Do you remember who was there that night? Who came over?"

There were people there that night, of course there were.

Her uncle sets down the drinks. "I ain't bring Billie here for this."

Carlotta doesn't appear to notice him. The bar goes quiet as it waits for the next song to play.

"I didn't bring her here for you to mess with her mind," he says.

"He was killed and you know it."

"You the only one who thinks that."

"It doesn't matter to me if I'm one or a hundred," Carlotta says.

"We leaving." He takes Billie's arm. "C'mon."

"I knowed the police protecting somebody," Carlotta says.

"Who?" Billie stands.

"One of they own."

CARLOTTA

IT'S FUNNY BUT THEY GOT THE SAME WALK, BILLIE AND DEE, FORWARD
on their feet like they can't get away fast enough. Cliff never
moved like that. He let the world see him. Maybe he picked
it up living in New York. He told her so many times about
meeting these two poets, serious poets he said, Henry and
Tom, who each showed him that to be a true artist he must
come into his blackness and make the collective experience
seen and heard. Cliff wasn't careful around white folks when
he came back. Her daddy said that it would get him killed,
no matter if they could vote now—because a black man in
the South walked around with a target on his back for every angry white man who felt life hadn't given him what he
deserved.

"What you think?" Donut is watching them leave out of
the corner of his eye.

"Dee hasn't even invited her to a family barbeque. He

might be her only uncle but the girl got cousins in the county."

"Why you think he brought her?"

"Better than having me going over to the house and see her by myself. He wanted to see what I said and what I didn't."

"You'd go over there?"

It is true that she hasn't been back to that house since the week after Cliff died. Miss Ruby let her in to collect her things. There was a child's shirt sitting folded at the bottom of the bed next to a teddy bear. Miss Ruby said Billie's momma had come and gone without a word. Even though Carlotta hated Pia, she had wanted her to come to the funeral so she could see for herself what Cliff's white ex-wife looked like. But wasn't that just like white folk not to give a black man respect even in death? So what if Jim McGee came and hugged Miss Ruby, that was like any good ole Boss man would do.

Carlotta could not remember how she got back to her sister's house that day. Only how she walked and walked looking for a sign from Cliff to say why.

"I'd go there if I had to," she tells Donut. "But I'm glad I don't."

Billie ain't as good-looking as her daddy. Even with those big sad brown eyes that don't know what they sad for. It's a shame the way the kids today know nothing about their own history.

The bar door opens and Dee comes rushing up to the table. "What the hell you saying that shit for? You said all you wanted was to meet her and I gave you that. Why you go on with that conspiracy shit?"

Carlotta shrugs to get at him. "She asked."

"She ain't know nothing to ask."

"She's got a right to know, a right to ask."

"It ain't about right or wrong. We are way past all that. You ain't ever understand. Not now and not then. Just let her be." He thumps the table. "That's what I'm asking." Dee turns to go.

"Is that what Cliff would want?"

He stops but doesn't turn. "You never knew what my brother wanted. You just never did." He walks out of the bar.

She hadn't been close to Miss Ruby until after Cliff's death. When they were first dating, Cliff's mother didn't approve. Thought Carlotta didn't wear enough clothes and was wild, going to too many parties. But it was only that she was nineteen and loved to dance. Cliff was the best thing that had ever happened to her back then.

Donut itches the top of his lip with a fingernail. "I don't know."

"What don't you know?"

"Best let it be, Carlotta."

"I couldn't even if I wanted to."

"Why not? Nothing good's gonna come of it, and we got a business to run. I got us that potential client in Jackson. Let it rest."

"I can't."

"Woman, why not?"

"It's not what God wants me to do."

"Oh Lord. Then don't do nothing but pray on it."

"Donut, ain't you ever met somebody special?" *Visionary* that's the word for what Cliff was.

Donut looks at her down his nose. "I have a wife and I think y'all are friends."

"What I mean is someone like no one you ever met in your whole life. Cliff wanted to lift our people up, lift up the folk right here in Greendale, but they ain't let him live long enough to do it."

"How was he gonna do that? You ain't ever say."

Carlotta takes a sip of her drink. "It don't matter now."

Donut declines a call, then looks at her. "If he hadn't gone and died young, it might not be so romantic. You never had the time to get acquainted with all his flaws."

"I never said he was perfect."

"All this mess gives me a strange feeling. Why you want to see that girl again? I can tell you ain't like her."

"I'm doing what I need to do for her daddy, for Cliff to finally get some justice."

"I don't need to tell you that you can't trust that low-down so-and-so."

She waves him away. "Dee ain't all bad. I knowed him a long time. He's just scared." It has taken thirty years, but something is happening.

BILLIE

IT COULD BE THE POLICE. HISTORICALLY SPEAKING THAT WOULD BE
an obvious possibility in the Deep South. Billie pushes back
into the soft leather of the seat. There must be some reason,
legitimate or convoluted, that Carlotta thinks so. Her uncle
brakes at the stoplight, still ranting about Carlotta's damn
conspiracy nonsense, only stopping for three seconds for a
"how you doing" to a guy hauling scrap metal in a beat-up
truck.

One of the deputies is dead: Oakes. One definitely alive:
McGee. But Roberts? He could be alive and even live in
town; it could be that she has passed him in the joyless fac-
tory lighting of Walmart and not even known it. She could
have stood in line, staring at the back of his head, tracing his
receding hairline, judging his items moving along the black
sticky belt, not knowing that the Little Debbies, white bread,
chocolate chip cookies, Mountain Dew, and rib eye steaks

belonged to the man who murdered her father. Though Carlotta didn't exactly say that those deputies did it, but that they knew who did.

"You hear me, girl?" The car slows as it approaches the driveway. "Folks like to believe all kinds of crazy shit out here in the Delta."

The sun is going down and the temperature dropping. She rolls up the window. "Why does she think he was murdered?"

"Carlotta think she knows more than everybody else."

"How serious were they? Her and my daddy."

"That was between them. I was just a kid."

When they pull up to the house, her uncle goes straight back to the trunk. As she steps out, he comes round and hands her a box. "These are some of Cliff's things. I thought you might want to have them."

She meets his eyes. But nothing in them says he knows about the chapter. "Thanks. Do you want to come in?"

"I gotta get back," he says.

A frenzied dog greets her at the front door. Inside, she opens the box and finds a few T-shirts, turtlenecks, a pair of corduroy pants, an old silver radio, and a few photographs of her father.

Under the rain tapping the trees, there are footsteps. Her uncle is walking the porch with a bottle of Jack Daniel's, listing like a boat with a bent sail. She comes out, hunched in a jacket, her neck hidden in her hair. "Hand it over," she says. She calls to Rufus and props herself up against the front of the house, trying to find raindrops in the dark.

"I'm sorry," she says.

He sits nearby, leaning his head back against the wood, watching the empty road made of dark mist. "Why you sorry?"

"I'm bringing up bad times for you."

"Worst time of my life. But you done nothing wrong."

He might not think so if he knew everything. She'll keep quiet about the chapter just a little longer. "Why were you named DeHart? You're the only person I've met named that."

"My daddy name me after DeHart Hubbard, the first African American to win a gold medal for the long jump in Paris, France."

"Really?" She passes the bottle back to her uncle. "What year was that?"

"All I know is it was before Jesse Owens." A small lizard climbs up one of the porch beams to the roof. "When I was young, we went to church twice a week. The Wednesday night prayer meetings were my favorite. Sundays were too long. I felt like God was with me and it felt good. When Cliff died, I couldn't go no more. Momma begged me. And I thought I would after some time passed, but I never did. I couldn't sit still." He exhales. "He cared about people. He mattered."

"I know he did, I know." She stands. "You've been drinking too much to drive tonight. Come inside. I might not have a couch, but I have an extra sleeping bag."

The rain echoes through the house, getting louder as Billie walks to the bathroom for a towel for Rufus. "Shit." Glass is all over the wet floor of her old bedroom. The window has shattered as if someone has taken a hammer to it.

Her uncle comes up behind her. "What happened?" He's in his socks.

"Stand back. Can you go around and get me the broom and a couple trash bags from the kitchen? I can tape it over for now."

She waits, but when he doesn't come back, she finds him on the back porch peering into the night.

"Did you hear it break?" His eyes are enormous.

"No, but it was already cracked."

"You seen anybody out here since that first night?"

She shakes her head. "It's okay, Uncle Dee, it was about to break. It's okay. Come inside, you're getting soaked." She leads him back by the arm. She locks the door behind him, then grabs the broom.

That night she sleeps with the sock next to her head. Nothing bad must happen to him. Not because of her.

DR. MELVIN HURLEY

HE NEVER FEELS EXACTLY HIS AGE. TODAY, IN PARTICULAR, HE IS NOT fifty-two. His years and quite possibly their collective wisdom go fluttering out of his rental car window as he drives past the downtown drugstore, which he has begun to frequent after lunch along with an elderly white man in a sweat suit and camo hat. They both prefer the register of a shimmering young black woman rife with blue eye shadow and God's love. But he's skipping the drugstore today and instead pulling next to a sedan in the dirt parking lot of an aluminum shed church, his thoughts on another woman. A woman he has not spoken to in over twenty years.

He folds his gum into a napkin then walks up to the church and knocks. There's no answer. He tests the knob. It opens and the shadowed air feels good. A woman hunched in the last pew turns to him.

She straightens. "Dr. Melvin?" Her short hair is side parted into loose curls above the purple silk of her blouse.

They shake hands. "I appreciate your meeting with me."

"This isn't my church," she says.

He nods as if he understands.

"I know the pastor. I've known him since we were kids. I'm a very private person, Dr. Melvin. I didn't used to be, but I learned." She turns to the front of the church, contemplating the bare wooden altar.

"Do you mind if I record our conversation?"

"No, no that's fine." Carlotta sits again, smoothing the ruffles along the front of her shirt. "Are you a Christian, Dr. Melvin?"

He takes out his tape recorder, setting it between them. "I was raised as one."

"He never leaves you, even if you've gone away from Him. I believe that. Before you came, I was sitting here praying you would be a good man." She purses her lips. "Until now, nobody has been interested in Cliff's death, in knowing what really happened. There were some of his artist friends who came down here when he first died and wanted to know what had gone on, but they didn't like to stay down here to find out. I guess it would have been different if it happened in a place like New York. But nobody, not even my own mother, would listen to me. I couldn't be here after that. I left the Delta for a little while. Then I came back like it seems all black folk do eventually and tried to let it go. But now she's here."

"I assume you're speaking of Billie?" Melvin moves forward on the pew, taking out his notepad. "As I said on the phone, she is helping me with the biography of her father's life."

"You never met him, did you?"

"Unfortunately not. I would love to hear you describe him?"

"He was so many things wrapped into one person. Handsome, so handsome. Full of charm. When he was with you, you felt like you was the only person in the world." She smiles. "My family moved to Greendale from Tchula when I was thirteen so I never met him till he moved back. Cause he'd lived in New York, I reckon folks thought he was slick. But this was his home, and he was at home here."

"Some people have described him as mysterious."

"He was a poet, ain't that what they supposed to be? He could be mischievous. That's for sure. Especially when he and Dee got together. They could make each other just about die laughing." She touches the thick gold bracelet on her wrist. "There are times when I wonder if it hadn't happened, would we still be together? But then I thank the Lord for my husband, who keeps me from doing things I shouldn't."

He can't resist. "And what does your husband think of your being here?"

"Like my mother used to tell me, husbands don't need to know every little thing."

Melvin smiles, hoping she doesn't hear his stomach rumble. He got her call just as he was ordering gumbo. "I'm thrilled you've decided to speak with me. In terms of the biography, I see your perspective as absolutely essential."

"She ain't safe here. I'm going ahead and say that on your recording. You seen the police report she got? I didn't need to. You know why? Because I already know who was there that night. I know who the suspects are. I don't know why I didn't do more at the time. I really couldn't tell you why. I suppose with the grief everything was too much to make sense of . . . there wasn't really any investigation. They was so quick to call it an accident and Miss Ruby was so scared she didn't want nobody saying nothing. She was from an older generation. She didn't believe in real justice for black folk. Not in this world." Carlotta presses her hands to her eyes. "See, here's that old place in me coming back." She fans her eyes. "I don't know for certain what happened that night. But I do know Cliff didn't fall over, hit his damn head, and die. And I knew the undertaker's wife. She said he had all kinds of bruises on him. His eye was swollen all the way shut."

Melvin's pen stops. "As if he'd been in a fight?"

She nods. "And it wasn't with no tree root."

"You believe that those three officers were responsible?"

"It could have been one of them, three of them, or five of their friends. All I know is it wasn't an accident. And you know what is messed up? Jim McGee was Cliff's best friend when they was kids. That's some kind of friend to do you like that."

ON THE DRIVE BACK TO HIS MOTEL, THE SUN IS A BAPTISM OF PINK. He left the church before Carlotta, who insisted that they leave separately. It remains to be seen who she imagines could be effectively watching. There's virtually nothing to hide behind here barring a smattering of thin trees across the field. The road itself is deserted except for one battered

THE GONE DEAD   165

red and white Chevy that turns right at the crossroad. There
Melvin puts the car in park and accordingly pulls out a CD
of Robert Johnson. Was there violence done to Cliff's body?
Are the perpetrators at large and circling Billie? Carlotta
certainly seems to think so. When he interviewed her so
many years ago, she said that it was not an accident, that
Cliff wasn't depressed. But if this is the case, then why on
earth would Dee allow his niece to occupy such a potentially
dangerous position? He must talk with Dee to get a better
sense of the current situation. He doesn't necessarily need to
gain Dee's approval any longer, though it would be nice. But
having Billie's cooperation makes the biography respectable,
possible. There needs to be at least one family member on
board, and now there is.

Perhaps the biography should open with a brief meditation on 1972. Something along the lines of . . . 1972, the
year that Shirley Chisholm, Ms. *Unbought and Unbossed,*
the first black woman elected to Congress, announced her
candidacy for president despite death threats, rampant sex-
ism, and outrage . . . (then some allusion to her practically
biblical visit to George Wallace's deathbed); the year that
the boundless provocateur Ishmael Reed published his pa-
rodic *Mumbo Jumbo* and his radical "Neo-HooDoo Mani-
festo"; the year that the cosmically sanctified Sun Ra and
the Arkestra filmed the Afrofuturist *Space Is the Place;* the
year that the tireless activist-icon Angela Davis was found
not guilty of murder; and the year that the largest Confederate (Lost Cause) memorial with Jefferson Davis, Robert E.
Lee, and Stonewall Jackson's visages was completed at Stone
Mountain in Georgia . . . though these are all American

references. Perhaps he needs to be more global in his scope? But in a sense these do point to the crucial tensions inform-ing and disrupting Cliff's process. He could mention that it's also the year Jimmy Baldwin published *No Name in the Street,* but to have another book may imply that black cul-tural liberation extends primarily into literature . . .

BILLIE

IN MEDIEVAL FAIRY TALES, THERE IS OFTEN A CHILD LOST IN THE wood. A monster lurks, perhaps an ogre or a witch, like the old woman who eats children in Hansel and Gretel, a story left over from the Great Famine of the early fourteenth century when the rains never stopped and summer lost its heat, a consequence of Europe's Little Ice Age.

As a little girl, whenever her mother spoke of it, Billie would picture Philadelphia covered with a layer of ice, a mountainous glacier where city hall stood, its citizens abandoning cars and umbrellas for spears and woolly mammoths, worshipping icicles because they were made by the sun, a star that ate the cold. Years later, her mother told her that the drop in temperature during the Little Ice Age simply meant disastrous rains, drowned cows, and ruined crops—not nearly as exciting. It meant that God was unhappy and you could not trust your starving fellow man, not alone in the woods.

At the bottom of the McGees' driveway, the hot grass tickles the skin above her sneakers, ghosts of past floods. She stands there until her bra strap cuts into a shoulder that's starting to burn. She walked here, wanting to rise out of the simmer of the afternoon, like a heat that makes the air ripple and blur.

She knocks. There is a black sedan and a blue truck in the drive. The doorknob turns and a man with a close-shaven silver beard opens the door, his thin hair light and sifted with gray. He must have been blond as a child, honey haired like Harlan. His blue eyes are made bluer by the red in his irises, the sharp cheekbones under his beard almost pitted.

"Hi, I'm Billie James." Her mouth tastes like hot pennies. "I'm looking for Jim McGee."

"Hi there, Billie, I'm him."

He's him. She feels for his face somewhere in her mind. It is not the one she would cast in the role of potential murderer. There's a weariness to the squint around the eyes, but not a smallness.

"Would you care to come in?"

She doesn't move. It's easy not to in this heat. "Do you remember me?" The words barely make it out of her mouth.

"Of course, though it's been a good long while and you look a little different. A little taller maybe." He smiles. "Miss Ruby used to bring you over all the time. She was real proud of you—you were her first grandbaby."

"Jim?" A woman's voice calls from deep within the house.

He turns. "I got it, Marlene."

Her scalp is itching with sweat, but it is important to be still, to miss nothing. "Can I talk to you about my father?"

"Of course. I'm not sure if I can tell you what you want to know, but come on in." He steps back, opening the door wider, the sun catching on his huge square belt buckle.

"Jim? Who is it?" The woman's voice again. Marlene? That name doesn't ring a bell.

"It's all right," he calls back as he leads Billie into the living room.

The woman comes up behind them. "Oh, I thought it was the mailman," she says, manicured hands on the hips of her white capris, expert highlights in her brown hair.

"Have a seat." Mr. McGee moves a newspaper folded on the armchair and sits. Billie takes the couch to the left of him. "Marlene, this is Billie James. Her daddy used to live in one of the places on the plantation. She's come to visit with me."

"Nice to meet you," Billie says.

Marlene smiles with no teeth, only thin fuchsia lips. "Nice to meet you too. You'll have to excuse me, I've got something in the oven. Jim, I could use your help."

He nods. "I'll be back there in a minute. Billie, you want something to drink? Coke or water? Though I warn you we only do diet these days." He glances at his wife as she retreats back into the kitchen.

"I'm fine, thank you. I hope I'm not in the way."

"Not at all. Not a whole lot going on now I'm retired. Though somehow she manages to keep me busy."

"I've been busier than I imagined trying to fix up the house."

"I'll bet. You need the name of a good exterminator? I know a guy you can trust. I'll tell him to give you a call if you like. If you mention my name, he should give you a good deal."

"Sure, thanks."

"How's the roof? I remember some of those old tenant houses had issues."

"I haven't noticed any leaks. But I'm not very observant in that way."

"Well, if you're planning to make a long stay you should get it looked at the way it rains here."

"I don't know that I'll be here much longer." She scoots forward on the couch, her elbows leaning on her knees. "So you and my father were friends."

"As boys, we were pretty much inseparable. But then as we grew older of course we sorta grew apart, and then he left Mississippi for college. And I was real proud of his accomplishments. Not that I'm any judge of poetry, but of what I read I thought they were something. But when he moved back here, life had taken us in different directions by then. I was married, starting to have kids, farming and working as a deputy. I'd see him around but I was real busy."

"And when he was found, you were there?"

"They called me out there." He rubs his hands together slowly, massaging his big knuckles. On one finger he wears a large turquoise ring. "Oakes and Roberts were there when I arrived. They were the first ones." He notices her looking at the ring. "My sister found out some years ago that apparently we have Choctaw blood in the family. She got me this. I don't know if I believe it, but she passed last year, so I figured I'd start wearing it."

"It's pretty." Hard to find a question that will tell her something she doesn't already know. "I met Sheriff Oakes."

"Bobby Oakes?" He scratches his beard. "That boy like

to tell you more than me. I'm sure he heard about it from his daddy."

"He mentioned the possibility of suicide."

He stares at the middle of the rug, seeming thoughtful, then says, "I wouldn't think Cliff was the type. But then I didn't have much to do with the case. The sheriff and the coroner did most of the work."

"Do you remember if there was anyone who had something against him?"

"He hadn't been back long, if I remember correctly. I think he had a girlfriend, but I don't think he was having any women trouble."

"Was there any tension between him and Oakes or Roberts?"

"Not that I'm aware of."

"Are you still in touch with Deputy Roberts? I couldn't find him in the phone book."

"Curtis?" He picks up his mug from the coffee table. "He's been dead for years. Some type of cancer. I suppose it'll get us all in the end. I've resigned myself to that much."

"Shit." No Roberts, no Oakes, just this friendly brick wall of a man. "Sorry."

"Doesn't bother me. I feel like I'm not being much help to you."

"Do you think he fell and that was it?"

"Sometimes there's no understanding these things." His blue eyes move from her to the mantel. "I had a daughter, Charlotte. She died a few days after she was born. Doctors never could tell us why."

"I'm sorry." She looks at the mantel but doesn't see any

baby pictures. "What about Curtis Roberts? What was he like?"

He leans back in the chair. "Curtis? Not much to tell. Curtis and me never got along. He was about as sharp as a butter knife. Dropped out in the eighth grade. He was with the department till he retired. I was only on it but three years. I wasn't precisely cut out to be a lawman and finally we had a good crop and I got my CPA."

"Do you remember if the possibility of homicide was raised?" She looks at him, but his expression doesn't change.

"I'm sure the sheriff looked into all the possibilities. It's hard to recall details now. But they must've had to rule that out." He glances behind her at the window.

She turns too, her eyes filling with sunlight. A car door slams.

"It's real good to see you, Billie. You doing good?"

She turns quickly back to him. "I'm doing okay."

They almost whisper.

"I was sorry to hear about your mother. I met her one time and she seemed like a good, strong lady."

"She was."

His eyes never leave hers.

"I found out I went missing," she says.

"You don't remember?"

"Not really."

"That's okay. You were real little." He leans forward. "You had a scraped knee. Remember that?"

Her hand goes to the knee still raw from the fall off her bike where a scab is just starting to form.

The front door opens. It's Harlan, clean-shaven, in a white

polo and wraparound black sunglasses, looking like the kind of preppy kid she never would've hung out with in high school.

"Hey there, son," says Mr. McGee but he is still looking at her.

Harlan walks halfway into the room. "I need to talk to you, Dad."

"Well, Billie's talking to me at the moment. Can it wait?"

"No, I don't think it can."

His father looks at him fully now. "Take your sunglasses off and act like you're somebody." He stands. "Billie, excuse me for a moment."

They disappear into the kitchen and she can't make out anything but the sharp murmur of voices. Something's wrong. She stands and puts her back to the foyer so she can take out the gun and check the safety. Whatever's happening probably has nothing to do with her. But Harlan didn't even say hello. The voices come closer and she jams the gun into the back of her shorts.

Mr. McGee comes back in, subdued somehow, almost sad. Harlan stays a few steps behind him, saying nothing.

"Harlan's just reminded me of something I need to take care of. Could we chat another time? Whenever suits your fancy."

"Sure." It's like he's been turned against her.

As Mr. McGee walks her to the door, his hand softly touches the top half of her back. "Thank you for coming by."

BILLIE IS WALKING IN THE DRY DITCH RUNNING ALONGSIDE THE MAIN road when Harlan's white truck appears. Nowhere to hide unless she lies down in the dirt.

Harlan pulls up, rolling down his window. "Hey." His stupid sunglasses are back on.

"What the hell was that?"

"You want a ride?" he says.

Crazy fucking white people. "Go away." She starts walking again, a spatter of rain hitting her on the forehead.

He drives alongside her. "My dad wants me to give you a ride home."

"That's nice of him. I like to walk."

"It's gonna pour down rain any minute."

She glances up at the darkening sky. "I like the rain."

"Why did you bring a gun to visit my father?"

She stops. He brakes. "What are you talking about?" she says, but the words are automatic, the gun is digging into her spine.

"It's sticking out the back of your pants. My mother saw it and about lost her mind."

"Why? People around here are armed all the time. Everybody's packing in Walmart."

"I ain't," he says.

A grasshopper leaps and spins in front of her shoe. "Well then, you're practically a pacifist."

"She thought maybe you had bad intentions."

"My intention is to protect myself."

"From my dad?"

"My uncle told me to be careful."

"My dad would never hurt anyone, especially not a woman." He takes his sunglasses off.

God, what's wrong with her, he is not even that good-looking. Certainly not her type. "It's weird to me that your mother would freak out. And you know what else? I have a hard time believing that you really didn't know my dad died in those woods."

He jerks closer to the window. "Is that what this is about? My family had nothing to do with that."

"You were a baby. How would you know?" she says as the sky opens.

"C'mon," Harlan says, pushing wide the door.

"Go home." The shoulders of her shirt are already soaked, mascara starting to drop under her eyes.

He drives next to her through the downpour until she reaches her porch, then he parks and gets out.

"Hey, you got something there." He points at her and hops up on the porch.

The dog is barking. "What is it?" She combs her fingers through her hair. "It better not be a bug."

"A little leaf." He walks up to her and picks it out.

"Rufus!" she shouts at the door. "You can go now," she says to Harlan.

"I did you the service of picking a leaf from your hair and that's what I get?"

"Very funny." She unlocks the door and lets Rufus out. He sniffs Harlan and leaps out into the rain. "Your dad was on duty when they found my father's body. But apparently he doesn't remember shit."

"Look, I think it's natural for you to be curious. But I know there are things he wouldn't do. My father is a good man. He doesn't drink anymore, he goes to church twice a week. People have a hard time talking about bad things that happened in the past, that's all."

"It didn't happen in the distant past to my great-great-grandfather. It happened to me, I was there."

"I didn't mean it like that." He sighs and looks out at his truck. "I better go. I'm working the night shift."

"Thanks for the escort."

"I could come by tomorrow, if there's something in the house you need help with."

"I have someone coming in from out of town."

He looks at the screen door as if they're lurking inside. "I better go." He walks down the steps, then turns. "Do you need the help?"

She shrugs, tired of the McGees, tired of having to fight for what she doesn't know.

"I could look the house over for you," he says. "Tell you what repairs you might need. I've done some construction work."

She opens the screen door and grabs the towel for Rufus. "Sure."

"I'll come by the day after tomorrow then?"

"Okay," she says.

At 4:00 A.M., Billie wakes. She wakes hungry, her mind whirring before she can catch up. She goes to the kitchen and makes herself a peanut butter and jelly sandwich so she can figure out what she thinks.

JIM McGEE

WHAT JIM McGEE CANNOT SAY TO BILLIE JAMES, CANNOT EVEN PUT into words in his own head, is: *There was a time I knew Cliff like I knew my own body. His walk. The way he breathed, the length of the air he took into his chest. When we were boys running through the brake, I could feel him move without looking. I always knew where he was and he always knew where to be. When I was in trouble, he'd come running. I'd look out my bedroom window, raw from a whipping, and I'd see him coming up the lawn. He wouldn't say nothing, just sit with me in my room. I loved Cliff, loved him. But our bond was nothing spoken. We ourselves wouldn't have known what to call it. It was just there like the trees, the birds, the fields—a naturally occurring thing.*

The girl looks like them both. Not that he remembers her mother much, but something about the shape of Billie's face calls Pia back. So it's true; deep down he has always believed that Billie would come back. Even if there is nothing any damn good for her here but an old shack and an aging drunk.

They spoiled him. Dee. Jim always thought that. But he was the baby of the family, even to Cliff who was almost old enough to be his father. More of a father to him than the man that was. A gift from God, Miss Ruby used to say. Dee grew up spoiled and did what he wanted, never making nothing of himself—not like Cliff who had the energy of three men—and now look at Dee, a broken-down man. But then Cliff brought too much on himself, wanted to change too much too fast. Nobody was ready for him and his damn photographic memory.

Jim remembers trying to get the little girl to sleep in Harlan's room, how Harlan was so small he was sleeping in a Moses basket by their bed. How Billie kept kicking her legs and sitting up, her eyes on him in the dark, checking that he was still there. She would roll away on the trundle bed then back, put her little butt up in the air like a caterpillar, kick her leg off and on the bed. You got the wiggles he said from the rocking chair. When he picked her up, she immediately put her head down on his shoulder. He walked the room, rubbing her back. A moment later he felt her little hand rubbing his. Children always know who to trust, his wife said. We better hope she don't know nothing about anything, he told her.

They hadn't had Charlotte yet, only their newborn son, but rocking Billie in the chair in the nursery he started to think of how one day he'd like a daughter. Marlene snuck in and hissed at him to lay the girl down, that she was asleep, but he still hadn't finished telling her with the way that he rocked her how sorry he was for what he hoped she hadn't seen.

Then she was gone, and the next night at three in the morning, he was so sleep deprived he started thinking of how they should have kept her and raised her, how they could give the child what she needed better than her unstable mother, how he could make it all up to her. He could hardly believe himself when he woke up in the sunlight next to Marlene feeding Harlan.

Then there was Dee's face at the funeral, how the sulk of it surprised him. Dee did not cry. Jim cried, but then he'd barely slept for the last two months. The day, the night—it was all one long shaggy thing. The boy was not a good sleeper from the beginning. Even now Harlan has nightmares.

His wife comes into the living room. He can tell by the pinch of her forehead that she is anxious.

"Marlene," he says, but that is all he wants to say. He shouldn't have let Billie leave like that. She deserved something more.

"I did it in a fever. I had to do something so I called Harlan. That girl was worrying me. She seemed so tense and when I saw she had a dang gun in her back pocket, I just about died. I thought she might have come here for a reason."

"Marlene, I've got my gun on me too."

"In a holster where it belongs, not hanging out in the open."

"She was nervous."

"She doesn't remember, does she?"

The question hangs in the air between them too long.

"No," he says, though he can't be certain. "Don't pitch a fit." Billie didn't seem to know him.

"Why in the world did she come back?"

"She's just curious."

"But why now? It was a long time ago."

But Marlene of all people knows that God is beyond Time. Isn't He? That's a question for the new pastor. "She's inherited her daddy's house," he says.

"You shouldn't have talked so much. You should have said you didn't remember anything."

"Don't fuss at me."

"She hasn't come here to live?"

"No, I don't think she has."

"I feel for her losing both her parents at so young an age, I do."

Marlene had him talk to a preacher once. He was a visiting preacher from out of town. Jim tried to talk, but he had to talk *around* things, and it didn't do him any good. But it shouldn't surprise him that there would be no relief.

"It was years ago now," he says for Marlene's benefit. "Whatever she might think she remembers isn't what happened."

"It's a disgrace. But you had absolutely nothing to do with what went on." Marlene is looking hard at the floor. "Do you want a sandwich?" she asks, her voice high and absent. "I made a couple from the chicken last night."

"That'd be nice. I'm heading back out to the fields directly."

"It's on the shelf in the fridge. Oh gosh, I think we're going to have book club here next week. Guess that means

I have to clean the good china. You know I always had a feeling—in my heart I knew she would come back."

"It don't matter now," he says, but he can see that it does. "Don't mention to any of them ladies that she came by. Not to your church group either. Last thing we want."

"We should have offered her something to eat," Marlene says pretty much to herself as she walks out.

DR. MELVIN HURLEY

BILLIE OPENS THE DOOR. "CURTIS ROBERTS IS DEAD."

Melvin steps inside, yanking off his prescription sunglasses. The room is awash in sun and loud music. "How do you know?"

"What?" She puts down her bottle of beer and moves away to turn the volume down on an old silver boom box. "Let's go out for doughnuts. I need sugar."

"Who told you about Curtis Roberts?"

"Mr. McGee. Oh yeah, I went to see ole Mr. McGee."

The house is much too hot for his blazer. His deodorant is already struggling in the day's heat. "I had imagined that we were going to see Mr. McGee together."

"Sorry. I couldn't wait. It was probably the wrong call." She picks at something gummed to the bottom of her T-shirt. "I brought my gun." There is dirt under her fingernails.

"I didn't— I wasn't aware you carried a gun." He strips off his jacket.

She laughs with little mirth. "It was my uncle's idea. He thinks some white supremacist smashed the back window. Clearly he didn't know I was raised as a pacifist. I did think that a gun would make me feel better. But maybe I wasn't really thinking. I've been meaning to practice out here sometime with some bottles, but I should've gotten a rifle I think. A rifle would feel more authentic, more Billy the Kid. And yes, so Curtis is dead."

"I hesitate to come across as preachy, but you do realize that most people end up shooting themselves or their family during a home invasion." He sits down on the armchair and rips a piece of gum from the jumbo pack in his jacket.

"I've heard something like that." Her Band-Aids are gone, all that is left is an angry blister between her thumb and forefinger that she keeps touching. "It's not like I know what I'm doing. Why are you gnashing on that piece of gum?"

"Sorry." He covers his mouth and spits it out.

"It's fine." She sits on the floor. "You were just chewing it so violently."

"I'm trying— I am in the middle of quitting smoking."

"Why didn't you tell me before? I had a boyfriend who quit. Well, who quit like seven times. It was terrible. For both of us. Chew away. Really."

"Thank you. I do want to take this opportunity to remind us both that we might never know what precisely happened to your father on that night."

She finishes her beer. "Especially now Curtis Roberts is dead."

"But I think we need to verify that this is indeed the case. Did Mr. McGee say anything else of note?"

"He remembered me, he said. Or that he'd met me as a kid. We didn't talk long because his son came home."

"It sounds to me like we'll have to have another conversation with him, a recorded conversation." He can afford to be forgiving today.

She itches a mosquito bite on her inner elbow. "I think I freaked them out."

"Perhaps I should come back when you're feeling better."

"I know I did."

"Well, it's very likely that you were probing into something most would much rather forget. One way to think about it is that at that time, and arguably still at this time, a black man's death wasn't all that important to local authorities. Which poses the question: Is the issue one of negligence? And did they investigate well, or at all? Or, as I've said, it's not inconceivable that in 1972 white police officers in the South were to some degree responsible for the death of a black man who had been a civil rights activist. Or, could it have been one of those cruel freak accidents?"

"It must be hard to end his biography."

"A Gordian knot of questions."

"I need another beer." She gets up and goes into the kitchen.

"I've never managed to produce a full draft," he says in her direction. "But like you I feel called here for a reason."

She leans in the doorway. "Atheist or agnostic?"

"The latter."

"Me too."

"I think that no matter what unfolds we can unearth much more about your father's life. The chapter you found gives us tremendous insight, but I want us to move forward on our quest, knowing that we may never know exactly what happened on that particular, tragic night."

"Right," says Billie, not looking at him. "So let's go now."

"Where?"

"To find out if Roberts is really dead. Come on, it's the South, everything closes round here by like three P.M. You drive, I'm drunk."

IN TOWN, THEY STOP AT A LOCAL GAS STATION, AN UTTERLY STORIED space with a surfeit of characters. Billie is fascinated by a cruelly tanned woman wearing a rhinestone belt sitting in her truck with the door swung open, scratching at lottery tickets.

"What do you think she'd do with the money?" Billie says.

The woman takes off her sunglasses, putting them atop her two-toned hair.

"Perhaps a cruise?"

"But what if she won like millions. Do you think she'd stay in Mississippi?"

"I'm afraid I haven't a clue."

"I think she would. She'd move into a huge brand-new house in the white suburb of Greendale and get a beach house somewhere on the Gulf."

After filling the tank, he waits in line holding five different flavors of gum behind a man in duck boots with a limp.

At the local library, they sit at a sanitized table under dark green lamps. Most of the patrons are crowded into the Children's section. They find a mention of Cliff in a condensed reprint of an obituary in the *Greendale Ledger* first published in the *Philadelphia Inquirer*. Billie says it was written by Pia. Curiously it makes no reference to the circumstances of Cliff's death. Only that they had "lost" and he had "passed," that he had written and had more to write.

He finds mention of the three deputies in wedding announcements, civic awards, as well as a few articles on the sheriff's election, but there is only one obituary for Oakes and nothing for Curtis Roberts, which has them posing the question of the day: Could Curtis Roberts still be alive? It's possible that Mr. McGee merely assumes Roberts is dead and has taken it for granted for so long that he believes it to be fact. On the other hand, there have been cases where a person with dubious dealings wants to be perceived as dead by anyone investigating said dealings.

On the drive to the county courthouse, old houses devoured by vines intersperse with flat fields dappled in sunlight. Billie points out her favorite trailer, a battered powder pink. Upon their arrival, Melvin requests Curtis Roberts's death record from the clerk who wears her glasses low on her nose, but here they discover that not only can they not access it as nonrelatives in the state of Mississippi, but that it doesn't seem to exist.

Back at the house, Billie drinks the last of the whiskey. Melvin drinks coffee and does not allow her to add even a drop because then he would want a cigarette.

"Mr. McGee specifically said it was cancer." She scratches her hair up into a bun. "Doesn't that mean he's lying?"

"He could be. Or it was what he'd been told. It's possible Roberts died in another state."

"We have to go see Mr. McGee again." She gets up. "It's not a bad walk."

"Why don't we call first? I find these things go better that way."

She sits back down, chewing her bottom lip. "But he's right there."

Melvin bends to place a light hand on her shoulder. "I realize that this kind of discovery makes it increasingly hard to be patient, but ideally we want him to feel that he can confide in us."

He never thought that he would find himself in the role of investigative journalist. Thus far in his career, dead men have always been dead. How to view the possible resurrection of Curtis Roberts? Does Curtis Roberts not want to be found, or does Mr. McGee not want Billie to find him?

He looks at Billie. "You know I've been thinking about the approach toward garnering excitement about the book."

"Do you think the rest of my father's memoir could be hidden somewhere in the house? Like under these floorboards? Some of them are already loose." Billie shows him a gap.

"Let's not rip the floor up just yet."

Rufus whines and Billie opens the door, following the dog out. In the silence left by their departure, Melvin rereads the chapter. He has always had the sense that Cliff was working on something before he died, that there was a book's worth of poems stashed somewhere, a draft away from perfection. But even when he and Dee were still on good terms, Dee had told him that there was nothing. And yet how was it that his ex-wife ended up with the chapter? Could Miss Ruby have sent it to Pia? It's possible that Pia had begun acting as a reader for him again. When they were together, she had been his first reader. She might only have had Chapter 2 if perhaps she'd already given notes on Chapter 1. But why hide it away, damning it to obscurity?

When Billie doesn't return, Melvin goes outside, finding her in the long grass just before the creek. Thank god he wore these old boat shoes and not his leather loafers. His shoes are already soaked in dew. He needs to just do it. Such things usually go over better than expected. She'll understand the way in which promotion works, the compromises, and besides it was his editor's idea.

She glances at him, almost expectantly, but then says, "Keep an eye out for snakes." She turns back to the water. "To be honest, I'm not really cut out for this place." The tip of her shoe pushes into the muddy bank. "I'm afraid of bugs."

"It's rather prehistoric out here." He steps over a suspicious-looking stick.

"It's getting to me." She wipes her eyes with the back of her hand. "Not the bugs. Everything else. It's mine to know, doesn't anybody get that?"

He stands abreast of her, trying to catch her eye, but she is gloomily pondering the swirl of ocher water.

"There's a blues song called 'Tallahatchie River Blues,' a

lament about the river flooding. There's this wonderful line that the woman—her name escapes me at the moment— sings about not being able to swim."

"Cheerful. Can you swim?"

"Yes, but not very well. I learned rather late. Though I do love the feeling of floating, being suspended." A mosquito whines near his ear.

"I learned in Canada." She picks up a long stick and pokes at the footprint she left on the bank. "My mom's friends owned a cabin up there and we drove up from New York and stayed with them one summer."

"Mattie Delaney, that's the singer's name."

"The water was cold, no waves, being a lake. It was nice. My job called today, wanting to talk about a meeting next week." She stabs the stick into the earth so that it stands upright. "I do have a life elsewhere that keeps me afloat. I'm using up all my sick days. I don't have forever to be out here."

"You told me that you write grants, correct?"

"Yeah." She looks around. "Do you see the dog? My parents would be disappointed. Rufus! They must have thought I'd have been something much more exciting coming from them." Rufus appears in between the trees. "But the kids almost never do, you know? They usually fizzle out."

Indeed, who could breathe under the weight of a genius father who was supremely brilliant and made a mysterious tragic exit?

"Maybe it's time for me to try something else, be a little less superstitious." Billie snaps her fingers for the dog. "I mean, I still don't like to step on cracks in the sidewalk."

Out with it. "I should tell you that I've published a short article on your father."

She traces a pattern with the stick across the ground. "Recently?"

"It comes out tomorrow actually."

The stick stops. "What's it about?"

"In a sense, it alludes to recent discoveries of Cliff's work. My editor thought that it would attract more support for the book, some of the requisite fanfare to make the splash we desire."

"But I thought you didn't want anyone to know about the chapter?"

"It doesn't say what the manuscript is about."

"Does it mention me?" She looks up.

Melvin nods. "Initially, it was going to run on an Africana studies website, but perhaps because of the enigmatic circumstances of your father's death, it was picked up by a few news outlets."

Her eyes bore a hole into him. "I haven't even told my uncle that we found the chapter yet."

"I should have come to you first, of course. I'm sorry. Things moved so quickly. It was a whirlwind. The *Greendale Ledger* is going to publish an excerpt today. Or, actually it must already be out."

"What? That's the local paper! I don't want everyone and their mother knowing I'm out here looking into his death."

"It strikes me—you don't feel that I've put you in any danger?"

Billie sighs, tipping her head back. "No. I don't know. I don't know what to think anymore."

"I'll make us a new appointment with Jim McGee."

She tosses the stick in the water. "I think I want to be alone right now."

"If you don't feel safe, I should stay."

She rolls her eyes. "It would seem that I'm safer without you."

BILLIE

IN THE LIBRARY WITH DR. HURLEY, SHE CAME ACROSS AN ARTICLE from a few years back about the passing of a former Mississippi sheriff whom the FBI had named a Klansman. Of course, the article did not mention the Klan. Dr. Hurley found that by doing a search of the name. The article listed all of the notable positions that the former sheriff went on to hold in the county and affirmations of his excellent service and courtesy. A good man, his son is quoted as saying.

There are so many Robertses in the state that Billie feels surrounded. Luckily there are only two in Greendale. Neither answered when she called from a sticky pay phone downtown. So she is taking the debatably logical next step.

It is a woman's name. Mabel. An old-fashioned one at that. On the drive over, swerving past roadkill, she keeps a Coke between her legs and finishes it while staking out the woman's house. It tastes like cops and robbers and Monopoly.

There's a car in the driveway of the modest bungalow. A few trees have started to bloom in the yard, but the grass is patchy. The pollen-coated porch swing looks like it's been a while since someone last swung. In the rearview mirror, Billie wipes off the mascara scattered under her eyes. No need to look demented. She's dressed with more care than usual: a relatively unwrinkled white button-down and jeans, her straightened hair slicked back in a bun. Vaguely professional except for the flip-flops and chipped toenail polish.

A woman answers after the second knock, filling the doorway with her bony but large frame lit by the TV screen.

"Are you Mabel Roberts?" The line is too practiced.

The woman scratches the back of her short gray hair. "Not if you're selling anything, honey."

"I'm not."

"And if this is about Jesus Christ, I've already found him."

"No, it's not that." Billie waves a persistent gnat from her face. "It's a little more unusual. I'm writing a book about my family and I think you might be able to help me. I think my family knew yours."

"Well, that sounds interesting. C'mon in, baby." Mabel slides on a pair of faded slippers by the door. "Want something to drink?"

"No thank you." Billie closes the door behind her.

"I just made sweet tea." Mabel sits down on a worn armchair and swirls her glass, making the ice clink. "Mine's got bourbon in it. The cheap kind but does the trick. Now what all about your family?" The news comes on. "Who's your people?"

Billie stands in the middle of the room as if giving a

book report. "The Jameses. I'm Billie James. They used to work for the McGees. I'm trying to find a man named Curtis Roberts who once lived in Greendale. I think he could be a relative of yours? He knew my father and I'd love to talk to him but I'm having trouble finding him."

Mabel sets her glass down. "Curtis? Oh honey, he's dead, God save him. Curtis was my older brother."

"But there's no record of his death."

"I got no idea what there is or isn't but he's dead."

"I know this is weird to say, but are you sure?"

The electric colors of the TV spill and twist over Mabel's face. "I think I'd know, wouldn't I?"

"Then maybe you could answer something else for me? Is it possible that your brother was involved with the Klan?"

"I don't think he was ever involved in all that crap." Mabel turns on a lamp.

Billie looks at the pictures framed on the wall. It's hard to make out their faces but there's none of an older man. "Can I ask if Curtis was married?"

"Yep, and divorced twice by the same woman, Sandy. Our daddy was the same. Curtis had just the one boy, that I know of, and he lives in Brookhaven." Mabel turns the volume down on the TV. "And you're saying Curtis was friends with your daddy?"

"I don't know what they were exactly. But your brother was one of the officers who investigated my father's death."

"Maybe I'm the one knew your family."

"Did you know a Cliff James?"

"Was he a black or white?"

"Black."

"Nope, don't remember him. You could try talking with the sheriff. When did he die?"

"Nineteen seventy-two."

Mabel sips her drink. "Oh, Curtis wouldn't have remembered nothing that far back. Nineteen seventy-two? Oh, you gotta let sleeping dogs lie, honey. No, my brother is dead."

When she gets back in the car, two men are parked next to her, tinkering with a motorcycle. If only she'd come back a few years ago, Curtis would have been alive. When she looks back at the house, Mabel is watching her from the living room window. But so what if Curtis is dead, that woman knows something. It would've been smart to have kept her drinking.

Billie pulls into a gas station and calls Jude to let her know she's alive. A woman in a tank top sits on the curb next to the pay phone, her face sore from crying. There's a can of soda between her bare legs and men's wraparound sunglasses propped on her head. The woman looks up as Billie passes.

"Are you okay?"

"Yes, ma'am. Do you have any quarters?" The woman looks at the road as she says this.

Billie takes out her wallet and goes to give the usual dollar, but then gives her five. Why not? What is it to her to be out five dollars?

"Thank you. I really appreciate it. I don't do this all the time. But my car's broke down and I have no money. Nothing to buy groceries for the kids."

"I believe you," Billie says and she almost sits down on the sidewalk next to the woman and cries.

JIM MCGEE

IT TAKES THE TWO OF THEM SOME TIME TO GET THEMSELVES UP THE driveway. They certainly are an odd pair: a short middle-aged black fella in a bow tie and a long-legged girl with her jean shorts sagging off her waist. Young woman he should say. Maybe she's not even that young anymore. They keep stopping to argue. Her hair is loose and falls straight down her back. Not curly like it was when she was a little girl. But he would know Billie if she was eighty.

When Jim answers the door, Dr. Hurley introduces himself and they both follow Jim into the living room and choose opposite sides of the couch, Billie practically sitting on the armrest.

"What can I do for you?" Jim asks.

Dr. Hurley glances at Billie but she says nothing, loud in her silence. Clearly stewing on something.

The doctor holds up a tape recorder. "Do you mind?"

Jim hesitates. "As a matter of fact, I'd prefer if you didn't."

"Of course. May I take a few notes?"

"Sure." Jim sits down in the armchair like he's taking the stand.

"Thank you for meeting with us, Mr. McGee. In our efforts to confirm Curtis Roberts's death, we've discovered that actually no records exist. I wanted to ask you if you thought it possible that he could be still alive?"

"First I've heard of it," Jim says. "I was told he had died a few years back."

The second day she was there, Billie came marching into the den singing "Frère Jacques" at the top of her lungs. She was trying to help him take a nap. She climbed up on the couch and had her elbow digging in his side by the time Marlene came running in.

"Who told you he died?" says Dr. Hurley.

"I was at a restaurant having lunch. I can't recall who exactly. More than one person."

"If he were to still be alive do you have any idea where we might find him?" asks Dr. Hurley.

"Buddy, I really couldn't tell you. I haven't spoken to him in years."

He and the doctor talk for a while about when he first met Curtis. Back when Curtis wore his hair short. They all did. White around the ears. Then there is no sound in the room but the grandfather clock, an old family heirloom, and the doctor scratching out his notes.

Billie rubs her knuckles against her closed mouth. Finally her hand drops. "When my father died and you found me, where was I?"

"On the porch." She was crying in the living room when he scooped her up.

"How long did it take to find me?"

"I don't know. I wasn't the one looking." This is true in a manner of speaking.

"Do you remember my grandmother putting a photograph of me up on the news, saying I was missing?"

The wind waves the branches and sun flickers across the coffee table as if the light itself is nervous. "With everything that was going on I think there was some misunderstandings."

"Did you see Billie's mother at this time?" asks Dr. Hurley.

"No, she wasn't at the funeral. It was Miss Ruby that identified the body. We called Cliff's daddy but he lived in Hinds County at that time. He did come, but he couldn't get here right away. Miss Ruby wanted to be the one." She asked him and his father to come with her and her brothers. He wasn't sure which broke his heart more, that moment or the one that would follow. As they escorted her down to the morgue, none of the other officers would speak to him. They wouldn't do much more than grunt and nod till he quit. It bothered him on the way in but holding Miss Ruby's arm on the way out nothing mattered. He swore the first mother couldn't have sounded worse, the first mother to ever lose a child.

"Does Curtis Roberts still have family in the area?" asks the doctor.

"A sister, and his son lives somewhere farther south, maybe Hattiesburg."

"What about his ex-wife?"

"Oh, I don't know about her."

Billie watches him like somebody hungry. He pretends to clean his glasses.

Dr. Hurley looks at Billie and nods, then stands. "We won't take up any more of your time." He and Jim shake hands.

Billie trails them as they walk to the door, but before she goes out she lowers her voice saying, "Please."

The rattle of insects leaks in from the open door and the hot air creeps over the threshold. If only he could tell her that he's protecting her.

"What is it, Billie?"

"Did anyone hurt him?"

"It was an accident, Billie." That's true too.

IN THE KITCHEN JIM POURS A CUP OF COFFEE GONE COLD. HE DUMPS the rest in the sink and rinses the pot out. The old house is quiet. He always imagined that it would be crowded with voices, kids scrapping over who gets what, lots of little hands looking for eggs on Easter. But that's not how it turned out.

Those two days of a toddler and a newborn were about as wild as it got. But then Pia flew into Memphis and drove down in a rental. Jim was upstairs when he saw her running from the car to the front door. Billie was in the kitchen, having a snack at the table with Marlene, Harlan was upstairs, finally milk drunk and asleep. Billie's hair was wet from a bath and dripping into the back of the smallest T-shirt Marlene could find, a pink one she'd bought at Orange Beach the summer before the pregnancy. Billie had been playing with some of the toys Harlan was way too little to use, but when she saw her momma, the light hit her face like sun on a mirror.

After a little bit, he got Marlene to take Billie in the living room and go read some kiddie books. She loved the *Busytown* ones and wanted to know what all the animals "dos." Pia wanted to talk in the foyer where she could still see Billie, but he told her it wasn't something they wanted a child to hear. It wasn't easy to peel Billie off her mother, but he had to talk to Pia alone, make sure she hadn't told anybody she was here, get her acquainted with the situation before things got worse. Already he knew he was coming under suspicion, but nobody had seen what he'd done except for Dee. Jim didn't know what kind of woman Pia was, her upbringing, if he could trust her to handle everything. He'd barely seen Cliff in the past few years, let alone this woman.

He'd been brewing coffee and he poured her a cup. She didn't want cream. She was a blonde, which surprised him because Billie's hair was dark, and she was tiny, but well made like a gymnast. That afternoon her face looked half dead from tears, her eyes pink. He didn't know where to start, what to tell, and what to keep.

"The child's gonna need lots of love and attention after what she's been through. The sooner y'all get away from this place, the better."

Pia nodded, listening to Billie try to jump on the couch in the living room. Then she talked about needing to go see Ruby and Dee, the funeral. "I was coming to get her in another week. I was going to take her to the shore. Cliff, he wanted—" Her voice cut out. She swallowed and looked away. "It was important to him that she learn how to swim."

There was no time to ease into it. "I mean you need to take her away now and never come back."

She stared like she couldn't see. He went to her as she groped for the counter. "What is it?" she said.

"Listen, I don't know what Billie might have seen, or what people might think she did. All you got to know is that her daddy got caught up in something and it's not safe for her here or for any of that family while she's here."

Pia leaned against the counter. "But she's a baby."

He led her to a chair at the kitchen table. "I don't know if I can put it past them. I just don't know. Come sit down."

"I need to think." She lay her forehead on the table, quiet for a while, then turned her face to where he was standing. "I thought this kind of thing was over, or that at least it was a little different now."

"It's different and it ain't. They get to say what happened."

"But you're one of them. You can tell people the truth."

"I've done all I can. More than I should. You have to go now."

She sat up. "I have friends who are lawyers."

"If that's your intention then you do so at your own risk and the child's and Miss Ruby's and Dee's. But I'm warning you, no good can come of it."

She banged her fists on the table. "I thought she was missing! They told me she was missing . . . A million horrible thoughts in my head, over and over until I heard your voice.

It was worse than death." She pressed her hands over her face, inhaled, then said softly, "What about Cliff?"

"I told you I don't know everything that happened, what he did."

"None of this is right."

"Right don't matter when you're dead. You do what you need to for your family." He waited. She wouldn't look at him at first, but then she said, "Where are her things?"

He called the TV station and they stopped running Billie's picture.

In the living room, Pia took her from Marlene. "Listen to Mommy," she said, holding Billie up in her arms. "What did you see at Daddy's house?"

"The policemen." Billie looked at him.

"Eyes," Pia said.

Billie looked at her. "Daddy went away."

"Where, where did he go?"

"He went to heaven."

Pia put Billie down and took her by the hand. "You've been telling her things."

"Well, we had to tell her something," he said.

He walked them to the car. Pia carried Billie like she was a smaller child, cupping the back of the little head and pressing it to her shoulder. Once she got Billie strapped in the back and the door was shut, he put a hand on Pia's shoulder. "Remember you were never here. We never met. I never told you nothing. And I will swear to all that on the Bible."

She looked at his hand. He let go. They looked at the

wrinkles he had left on her beautiful silk shirt. He wanted her to listen. He wanted her to believe he was a good man.

"You're doing the right thing," he said.

She snorted. "Neither of us are willing to do that. I just hope he can forgive me."

"There's nothing he can't do."

She looked at him with narrowed, furious eyes. "Not god, Cliff."

DR. MELVIN HURLEY

BILLIE IS NOT AT HOME. BUT THEN NEITHER IS THE DOG, AND WHEN he calls her phone it goes straight to voice mail. She's never missed one of their meetings. He has always found her inside with a book or sitting out here on the porch in a wrinkled T-shirt that would have made his mother cringe. Of course, it's possible he's mixed up the time, though he doesn't believe so, and now that he thinks of it, she always answers his calls. Even lately when she's been upset with him about the whole article snafu.

For a while he sits in the driver's seat with the car turned off and the door open, taking out an essay reexamining Addison Gayle's *The Black Aesthetic,* a book that coincidentally came out a week before Cliff's death. If this one is a flop, he has Isaac Hunley's essay "The Formation of the Outside Agitator" as a backup.

Of late there has been some suggestion that he should

make his much-discussed essay "The Art of Reclaiming Blackness: The Radical Desire of the Black Arts Movement" into a book. But with this project coming back to life, and something else, a pervasive little whim . . . after Billie mentioned Mae Cowdery, he started thinking about all of the fascinating women writers in and around the Harlem Renaissance who have been largely forgotten or excluded or even silenced, and how he could begin by developing a course that would focus primarily on Jessie Redmon Fauset, Gwendolyn Brooks of course, then Marita Bonner, maybe take a look at one of Regina Anderson's plays, read Esther Popel, whom he knows absolutely nothing about (but what a name), Pauline Hopkins, Nella Larsen obviously (though technically both she and Zora Neale Hurston have been "rediscovered"), the reclusive Angelina Weld Grimké (why exactly do so many of these women end up recluses?), and then wouldn't it be interesting to include Nat Turner's granddaughter, Lucy Mae Turner. Oh, and perhaps Pauli Murray could be worked in at the end as a bridge into the civil rights era? A visit to the Schomburg Center would certainly be in order. He's been away from New York for far too long.

It could eventually become a larger project. He's always had a penchant for the unknown lives and obscured works of marginalized writers. As a kid, he wanted to be a renaissance man. It was something his father used to say before going out to his card game. His father, though entrepreneurial by nature, tended to accept that his eldest son preferred going to the library on a Saturday as opposed to playing baseball.

An hour passes, but the landscape is silent except for the

occasional truck or bird. He can't help but feel that something has gone terribly wrong.

Perhaps he's committing another faux pas, but it's not a question of whether or not he should make this call but when. Billie hasn't done it, he knows. There are so many questions that are likely to go unanswered, that have been buried with the dead, but a little information would move them much closer to sketching out a more accurate picture of what happened.

The phone rings, a man answers. "Yes?"

"It's Dr. Hurley. Please, don't hang up. This is vitally important. I can't find Billie."

There's a pause and then Dee says, "I ain't her keeper."

"She knows that you're mad at her about the article. I sincerely hope no one has harassed you over it. I want you to know that it wasn't her doing, and that she had no idea it was being published until it came out, and that she was quite upset on your behalf."

Dee sighs. "I ain't mad. When's the last time you seen her?"

"Yesterday. But it's unlike her to miss a meeting."

"You two best friends now?" Dee clears his throat. "I don't see that there's much to worry about. She's grown."

Melvin waves away a mosquito dancing toward him. "So I shouldn't be concerned that anyone would have done something—run her off the road for instance?"

Dee does not respond.

Melvin climbs out of the car, pacing the length of the porch. "I want to tell you something about our discovery.

The chapter the article alludes to is a Chapter Two of an unpublished work, which leads us to believe that there is a Chapter One, but what also is of importance to me is that we found it among Pia's belongings."

"My momma sent it to her."

"But were they, were they on good terms?"

"My mother was a saint. She sympathized with Pia because Cliff left her and my momma knew how that felt."

"Did you ever see the first chapter? Does it exist?"

"Listen, Doctor, you said yourself it ain't safe for Billie round there. If you can get my niece to go on back to Philly, then I will see if I can help you out with that chapter."

Melvin stops. "Why would I—why would I believe that you would do that now after all your resistance?"

"Don't worry about whether or not to believe me, man, just get her out. It's time."

BILLIE

THEY'VE BEEN TO THE DOG PARK BEFORE. TODAY AS SHE PARKS IN the gravel outside of the tall chain-link fence, there are no dogs in the open field. It is starting to rain ever so slightly and the overcast light is oddly sharp. Rufus paces the backseat and when she lets him loose, he takes off, tongue flapping. She hangs the leash on the fence near the entrance and tucks her bun under her baseball cap, then walks deep into the field, dodging hardened dog poop, a filthy tennis ball in hand.

She tosses the ball, lobbing it wildly. Soccer was her sport and she was always bad at throw-ins. A truck pulls up next to her car. Rufus abandons the tennis ball and races across the field. She walks after him so he won't crowd the entrance, but the truck doesn't have any dogs in it. Maybe they're lost. Rufus barks, duped into excitement. Maybe they're pulling over to make a call.

"Rufus!"

Two men in sunglasses and ball caps get out of the truck. Both heads turn to her. They want her to see them seeing. She stops. The dog park is secluded. It is down a gravel road lined thick with trees. There are no houses, no other roads. One man goes to the back of the truck and takes out a rifle. She sprints forward. If she gets to the gate before them, she can try for her car. Whatever they want, anything is better than being trapped. Rufus trails the men along the fence, barking. But the one with the gun gets to the entrance first, jabbing at the dog with the butt of the rifle. Rufus bears down and snarls.

She slows, tripping against her own feet. "Shit. Rufus!" She fumbles for her phone. "Rufus, come!"

The 911 dispatcher answers. "What is your emergency?"

"I'm at the dog park—shit—I don't know what it's called! There are two men. One has a gun. Rufus!" The man swings the rifle at Rufus, who refuses to back down, the other man laughs. "Stop it! Leave him alone!"

"What is your full name?"

"Billie James."

"What is the dog park near? Can you give me a town?"

"I don't know! Greendale, Greendale."

"Stay on the line. Are you able to leave the park? Ma'am?"

"No," she says. "They're coming this way."

"Are you hurt? Tell me exactly what is happening."

The man with the gun steps back and shoots. Billie screams, forgets the phone. Rufus drops like a toy dog whose batteries have gone dead. Both men look at her. She drops to her hands and knees, looking for the phone. Forget it. She scrambles up, running right toward the fence. She can climb it, jump down, and run just run. The bigger man, the one without the gun, is coming after her. Her thighs burn. She hurls her body toward the fence, the heat of him behind her. Mud splashes up her ankles as the fence looms closer. She can almost touch it. A hand wrenches her shoulder back and smashes her to the ground. Her tongue fills her mouth with blood. She can't breathe. Hands drag her up by the hair. She tries to rip them off and the man whacks her in the face. She curls into a ball on the ground. He kicks at her hands. She howls and pulls in tighter. Pain cracks the top of her head. A white pain too big to stay inside her body. The man yanks her up, spitting in her face. "Go home, you fucking bitch." Then the other is there, gangly with a young man's beard, pressing the barrel of the gun into the side of her head. Far away, her phone is ringing.

"Please don't."

They laugh. Their teeth, voices unknown to her.

"What do you want?" she screams.

"Leave us the fuck alone." The rifle drops and a fist hits her face.

HOW LONG HAS SHE BEEN LYING IN THE RAIN, FACE UP TO THE OPEN sky. *Mom.* The sky leading into the stars but there is bitterness in the white. *Mom.* She turns her head; a wave of nausea buries her. *Is she there?* She vomits. It's better to lie still. Her right hand gently discovers her chin. There's something wrong with the other hand. *Is she here?* It's better to sink into the wet. The puddle is eating her hair into cold, tight curls. A sound is close. Someone crying. Everything is dripping: the rain, the birds, the sirens in the distance.

Rufus. It is agony to roll over and push herself up onto her elbows. She stands, half crouched, and drags herself to him.

"Hey boy." His belly is dark red fur. She kneels and strokes his head. He whimpers. She carefully pulls her shirt off over her head, dabbing at his stomach until she sees the mouth of blood, and presses her shirt to it. "Hold on, boy. It's gonna be okay." But it really isn't, is it?

The sirens are getting louder. A white ambulance barrels down the road and into the parking lot, the red and blue lights falling over each other onto the trees.

THEY'VE KEPT HER OVERNIGHT TO MONITOR HER CONCUSSION, THIS mild brain swelling that makes her the one in the hospital for a change. A trip to the bathroom with her IV shows her a half-closed eye, a split bottom lip, a shorn patch on her head for the stitches, and blood-colored cracks over her nose. Let not this body be a true reflection of the self.

In all of her dreams, she is younger. The nurses call her honey and child. They want her to tell them how things are at home, assuming she's been beaten up by a father or a boyfriend. A cop has come in to ask questions, so it must have gotten back by now to Sheriff Oakes. If he knows the two men, then they know she's here. They could work in the hospital as orderlies, their girlfriends could be sitting at the front desk.

As the drugs wear off, the pain becomes electric, snapping whenever she moves. Her mother always said that pain is trying to tell you something. But what did it tell Mom other than that she was dying fast.

Unwise to go back to the house. They must know where she lives. But she needs to get the gun, some clothes, at least her father's manuscript. The best thing would be a motel. Somewhere surrounded by other motels, strangers, security cameras, out-of-town plates.

And then? Hard to think now that her brain's been bounced off the sides of her head. She feels wrung out, her thoughts taste of chalk. The officer looked sympathetic. But he was young. Probably a rookie. No leverage. Think, think, think. What next?

She just screamed and cowered and cried like a helpless fucking thing. Didn't fight for her life like the dead women do on crime shows with their defensive wounds. During the Black Death, some Christian towns blamed their Jewish community, so they massacred them, sometimes burning them in their houses. Jewish women threw their children in the fire, then themselves rather than renounce their faith.

Some coffee, some pills, and she'll be okay. She goes into the bathroom, takes her dirty clothes from the plastic bag, turns her dirty shirt inside out, and puts it on—it's black so the blood doesn't show. She scrapes what mud she can off of her jeans and shakes her caked shoes over the trash can. There's not much to be done about her hair, since she can't get the stitches wet.

A taxi drives her to the dog park. She tips the driver extra to wait until she gets in her car. There it is, right in the middle of the scrubby grass. So ignoble of a spot on which to almost die with Rufus, the one living thing she was meant to take care of.

She maps three different routes home and takes the most circuitous. When she's satisfied that she's not being followed, she stops at a white-fronted doughnut shop and gets a glazed doughnut and large black coffee so she won't be lulled by the sunlit monotony of the road. She calls work and tells them that she was in an accident. That will buy her more time. Just a little more is all she needs, maybe all she can survive.

Back in the car, she drives slow, letting the pickup trucks high on fat wheels overtake her. At Walmart, she keeps her sunglasses on and adds a baseball cap, but people still stare at her torn mouth, taped fingers, the bruises on her arms and neck. She drops off her prescription and waits in a fog. All that matters is that she can see straight.

The road near the house is empty except for a few birds on a power line and the same rusted-out tractor at the edge of the field. Billie packs her suitcase and puts the gun in her pants, then she fills a box with a few books and her father's manuscript and loads it into the trunk. For a few minutes she rests in the car, locking the doors and closing her eyes.

The finger splint on her left hand rests on the top of the steering wheel. At least it wasn't her right. It's the ring finger that's broken, bulging against her middle finger and fractured pinkie. She turns on the car and catches herself in the rearview mirror. Maybe she should wear an eye patch. The squeeze starts in her chest, pushing into her throat. But it's not time to cry. It's her move. Hopefully nobody will burn the house down.

THE CAR IN MABEL'S DRIVEWAY IS THE SAME AS BEFORE. SHE PARKS and sticks the gun in the front of her pants, wincing as it nudges her cracked ribs. If she tucks it a little lower she can pull her shirt over the bulge. Outside, a heavy breeze promises thunder.

Mabel answers the door on the second ring. Billie pushes up her sunglasses. "Hello."

Mabel says nothing at first, her mouth falling open a little. "What are you doing here?"

"I thought I'd drop by."

"I got nothing to say to you."

Billie's hands are shaking but the anger is warm around her shoulders. "I just want you to tell them that it's not over, that it has never been fucking over. Because I don't want there to be secrets between us, Mabel. I want it all to come out."

Everything about Mabel is suspended: the tint of her glasses purpling in the light, the crease of her cheek running alongside her mouth, the layers of red stippled softness under the gold chain around her neck.

"Don't be a dumbass and go home, girl."

"This is my home now," Billie says, walking back to the car.

AT THE MOTEL, BILLIE TAKES A NAP, SLEEPING TOO LONG AND BADLY, waking often but unable to get up. They'll be coming any minute now through the shabbily ornate lobby with one sad small aquarium behind the beige front desk. The motel could be anywhere with a dollar store on the left and the highway on the right and for this reason it almost feels safe.

She pulls her sleeping bag over her legs and adds another pillow behind her back. There's a bottle of gin and a paper cup of black motel coffee on the nightstand next to her, a bad combination, but she needs both. The liquor store didn't carry tonic so she has to drink the gin straight. Not enough to get drunk but just enough to soften the fist in her stomach. At least she's showered and in clean clothes, her only ones. The plan was to go to the Laundromat after the dog park, not to have a cut on her temple held together by three stitches. Or her blood in that shitty grass. That literally shitty grass.

Her phone rings occasionally. Jude or her boss. Voices from that other life. Not this one of gin and blood and a dark room choked by the ghost of cigarettes.

Rufus is at the veterinary hospital. The bullet didn't puncture any organs, but he lost a lot of blood. They said they had a dog once who was shot in the head and he was okay. Between the motel and the vet, money is tight.

There is a knock. Billie climbs out of bed. There's no time to clean up the back of the room where the counter is littered with toiletries and sink spattered with blood. She looks through the peephole and opens the door.

Carlotta looks her up and down. "They sure got you good."

"Thanks for coming." Billie steps back.

Dr. Hurley follows Carlotta in, stopping to gaze upon her. "Didn't she warn you?" Billie says.

"I don't know what I was imagining but it wasn't to this extent."

"It's all right," Billie tells him, going back to sit on the bed.

Dr. Hurley slumps in the heavy armchair by the window whose curtains are drawn tight against the sun. Carlotta sits at the desk by the TV, leaning down to open the minifridge, and taking two cans of flavored seltzer out of her purse. "You want one? I'm trying to quit soda."

Billie lifts the bottle of gin on her nightstand. "I've got this."

"Is it wise to be drinking?" Dr. Hurley asks.

"No, but it helps."

"Aren't you on painkillers?"

"This is for my feelings. Don't worry; I'm only on like triple ibuprofen or something."

"Have you spoken to the police?"

Carlotta snorts. "They ain't gonna do nothing for her if it's their friends who did it."

"I talked to the police at the hospital, but Carlotta's right that I don't think I'll hear much from them. Anyway, I already know who did it."

"You recognized your attackers?"

"Not exactly but I can make an educated guess. So I should tell you that two days ago, I went and saw Mabel Roberts, Curtis Roberts's sister, and asked her about him." Billie waves his protests away. "I knew you'd want to call ahead, and I thought if I just appeared maybe she'd be surprised into letting something slip. Anyway, when I talked to her, she insisted that Curtis was dead. Then those two goons showed up the next day at the dog park. I guess subtlety is not the Roberts way. They didn't take my wallet. They didn't rape me. Who else would attack me in broad daylight when I'm with my dog? It was someone in that family."

"Did you tell all this to the police?"

"I don't know that Sheriff Oakes isn't on their side. He knows them and he doesn't know me. Besides, I can't prove anything."

Carlotta is picking a piece of lint from her slacks. It descends onto the colorless motel carpet. "Dee don't live here no more so he should be okay. They don't know where he's at. But we'll have to tell him what's up soon."

Billie takes a swig of gin. "Oh shit, I left Mr. Hopsen's lawn mower outside. I hope nobody takes it."

Carlotta looks up. "How you know Jerry?"

"I met him a couple weeks ago at a garage sale. I guess you must know him too."

"From back in the day."

"Billie, I don't think that you should stay in town," Dr. Hurley says. "This has all escalated to a simply astonishing level."

"They scared because she's close to knowing the truth," Carlotta says.

"I'm scared too if indeed we are supposing these men to be relatives of Curtis Roberts. What will stop them from doing worse?"

Carlotta crosses her legs and smooths her slacks down to her ankles. "All they have in this world is they anger. I've known white folks like them my whole life. But Cliff deserves justice. I don't know how he got mixed up with Curtis Roberts but he must have. Curtis was known to be rough on black folks, beating them up in jail. But that's all I ever heard bad about him."

The gin is making her dizzy. Billie eases herself up to fill a glass of water at the sink, then sits back on the bed, scooting back and leaning against the headboard. "You don't have to stay, Dr. Hurley. Or at least you don't have to be involved in what comes next."

"Billie, if you would go back to Philadelphia, I would gladly do what's necessary in terms of starting the process of seeking justice."

She looks at him. "Everything that's happened needed to happen so that I can find Curtis Roberts. And that's what I'm going to do."

CARLOTTA

SHE DIDN'T SAY NOTHING TO THOSE TWO BACK AT THE MOTEL. IT MAY be that they need to get Dee to open up. Lord knows she's been trying for years. But first she is gonna go see Jerry Hopsen.

Ever since Billie mentioned his name, she's had a bad feeling. What's Jerry doing talking to Cliff's child? Cliff and him hadn't gotten along since the fifth grade. Only reason they ever talked was because Cliff was close to Sheila, who could have done better. Never knew why she picked stubby ole Jerry Hopsen. That's what the girls said about him—that he had a chubby ole stubby dick. Carlotta ain't even like to remember that in case she starts to picture it.

As she pulls up to his house, he's sitting out on his porch. When he realizes who it is, he waves. She hasn't been here since Sheila died. She walks up the drive but doesn't step up on the porch.

"How you doing?" he says.

"Just fine." She puts up a hand to shield her eyes from the sun. "You?"

"Can't complain."

"How's the kids?"

"Sandra's real good. She started working a new job up in Grenada. Marcus is the same."

His voice changes whenever he mentions the boy. He never did understand that child. How can anybody be surprised when a boy watches his mother get eaten up by cancer and his best friend die out on the street that he might hurt and act hard, be angry. She always liked Marcus herself. Nothing like his daddy. Not secretive at all. Feels deep Sheila would say.

"You seen Cliff's child come back?"

"Sure did. In fact, she came by the other day."

"She come looking for you?"

"Naw. She came by to take a look at a yard sale I was having. You seen her?"

"Dee brought her over."

"Don't sound like something he would do." He rubs his knuckles. Still wearing his wedding ring. "You know what happened to the girl? Other day I come by to get the lawn mower she borrowed and it seemed like she was long gone. She ain't answer my calls either."

Carlotta steps into the shadow of the house. "She's not trying to take your old lawn mower."

"I don't know why she's here when her family's gone and there ain't no jobs to be had." He picks up the beer can sitting next to his chair. "No good is gonna come from her hanging around here."

"How you know?"

"Ain't rocket science."

"Maybe you right. I heard she got beat up by two white boys."

He looks down at his beer and sits back, saying quietly, "I ain't heard nothing of that."

"You know anybody who would do that? And shoot her dog? You know anybody want to hurt Cliff's daughter?"

"All I know is that it's a God-given shame."

"You know I been thinking back to the night Cliff died, how we were supposed to go out. But then he said he couldn't meet because he had to meet you at Avalon."

"We done talked about this in the past. And he went on home just fine after that." He's acting a little loose, like he's been drinking for a while.

She gets up on the porch so she's looking down at him. "Tell me again what y'all talked about."

"I don't recollect what got said. It was about Sheila."

"That I can believe. And nobody was looking for Cliff that night? Was he worried about anybody?"

"You've asked all this before and I'm telling you the same answer, no."

"Was he worried about some white men? I ain't never asked you that before."

"Listen, whatever went down with Cliff had nothing to do with me."

"Well, now that's interesting"—she nods—"interesting you would say it like that."

He looks up at her. "I'm saying I got no damn idea what did or did not happen to the man."

"I wonder what Sheila would say about you. About you sitting up there lying through your damn teeth." She turns and walks down the steps.

He stands. "Ey I told you, Carlotta, it's got nothing to do with me."

She stops, looking back. "You right to worry about the girl. Because whatever happens to Billie is on you."

LOLA

LOLA IS SITTING ON THE BACK BUMPER OF HER CAR, CIGARETTE IN hand. The motel parking lot is so hot that nothing wants to move, not even her smoke. Billie comes down the balcony steps in running shorts and a hoodie pulled low, but it can't hide her left eye slick and bruised.

"There are four lights in this town and I hit every one. Sit down, gal."

Billie sits, then jumps. "The car's hot." As she scans the parking lot, she trips on a pair of drugstore flip-flops too long for her feet.

"You remember what those dudes look like?"

Her eyes flicker to Lola. "Forever. Of what I could see of their faces. How can you sit on that?"

"I am beyond heat. Do you always have this much drama in your life? Between you and Martha Stewart getting arrested the world is going to hell in a handbag."

This gets a smile out of Billie. "What happened to Martha Stewart?"

"Bitch got caught. Insider trading." Lola puts out her cigarette. "Look, I love Mississippi. And I will always love it. Nobody's gonna take that away from me no matter how ignorant they act. But I wasn't surprised. Now the dog did surprise me, but not what they did to you. The Robertses wanted to scare you."

"Well, they did a good job."

Lola picks her bottle of Coke up from between her sandals. "But you came here because that's what God wanted."

"What if I don't believe in God?"

"You don't?"

"Well, I don't not believe. Oh man, why does everything around here have to be so heavy?"

"It's the floods, all the times the river overflows. This is all was meant to be a flood plain. The Atchafalaya wants to swallow the Mississippi and the Mississippi wants to join it. So this place is all longing and water and ghosts. Those shoes are too big."

"It was the smallest size they had. You should meet Dr. Hurley. He talks about the Atchafalaya too."

Lola eyes her. "And you got blood on that hoodie."

"Oh shit." Billie pushes back the hood and pulls at her collar. "Is my nose bleeding? This is the only one I have with me."

"Tip your head up. Don't look like it. Maybe you should go on back to Philadelphia."

"Maybe I should be out there looking for them. Riding around with a baseball bat."

"That ain't you." Her cousin does not need to be going anywhere.

"Maybe it is now." Billie strips off the hoodie. "This is too hot anyway. I thought you said God wanted me here?"

"I didn't say for how long." Lola can smell the liquor on Billie's breath. "You talk to the police?"

"At the hospital. I shouldn't have bothered. I didn't get the license plate."

"They might call you in to look at mug shots." Lola offers her the Coke.

"I doubt it." Billie shakes her head.

"What about the FBI?" Lola sets the Coke down on the asphalt between them.

"I think the dog park is state property."

"I meant wouldn't this qualify as a hate crime?"

"They didn't say anything racist to me though."

"They ain't need to—it was racially motivated."

"It doesn't matter." Billie picks up the Coke. "The important thing is that I am almost certain Curtis Roberts is alive and guilty of something. I just have to find him."

And not get herself killed. "Don't go back to his sister's house. That woman ain't gonna give you nothing but more trouble."

"No, I'm done with her for now. I'm thinking the next step is to go back to Mr. McGee. If he sees my face—"

"He saw your daddy's face and he didn't do nothing good." Lola opens her purse for another cigarette. "What about the son that likes you? He know anything?"

Billie runs her thumb over the rise of her bottom lip. "I don't know. We're not that close."

"Quit messing with your mouth."

Billie's hand drops. "If I die, you can have my car."

"You stupid."

"You can sell it. It's gotta be worth something."

"Billie, stop it."

"For your debt." Billie laughs.

"I can stay here tonight if you want company."

"No, no, you better not. Get back to Memphis."

"Those fools don't know you're here."

Billie looks down at the bottle. "Shit, I think I finished your soda. Hey, what's going on with your boyfriend?"

"Oh, I don't know, it's over." And that's basically true now that she's said it.

"You broke up?"

"I don't think I need to—I can just tell him I'm busy."

"You don't seem upset."

"I've been upset for months, but with all that's been going on, I don't know, I'd rather be alone if it's not something real."

"You're going to end up a bachelor like me."

"I don't want none of that monk shit. I just don't want to waste no more of my time."

Billie raises the empty plastic bottle. "I toast you."

"You ridiculous. Let's go up. You still want takeout?"

"I guess. I'm not that hungry." Billie watches a truck pulling in, waiting until a couple gets out with their little dog. "I don't want you to stay here for too long." She turns back to Lola. "You think I'm doing the right thing, right?"

"Our folks are survivors of the terror of segregation. This

is part of your inheritance, it's up to you what you want to do with it."

Billie smiles. "But is God with me?"

"That depends on what you do."

Lola follows Billie up the motel steps. Let this not be the last time she sees her. Not again.

DR. MELVIN HURLEY

THIS IS THE QUINTESSENTIAL MOMENT IN WHICH TO HAVE THIS CRU-
cial discovery. His theory about Cliff's lost work is now not
merely conjecture. Not only that, but he himself has become
much more of a character in the narrative than he could
have ever imagined. His firsthand observations are now a
vital part of the biography. Of course, he cares what happens
to Billie, but to see the story turn this corner is truly something to behold.

He pulls into the parking lot and cuts the engine. Of
course he vaguely assumed that the apartment complex
would be run-down, but he didn't picture this battered vestige of a motel. A man, who must be Dee, is on the second
floor balcony smoking. Melvin steps from the car and Dee
nods down at him.

They meet on the balcony. The cigarette smoke is heav-
enly. "I appreciate you meeting me, Mr. James."

As they shake hands he remembers that they are not actually that far apart in age. He is a little older than Dee, but Dee looks like the older man.

"Don't have long." Dee takes a drag on his cigarette.

"I understand so I will cut to the chase and say first that thus far Billie is resistant to returning to Philadelphia."

"She ain't still staying up at the house, is she?"

"Not at the moment, no." Melvin tries not to stand downwind. Two weeks, almost three now. "I doubt very much that she will leave until she sees the elusive Curtis Roberts." He would be back down to zero if he had a cigarette now. All his suffering in vain.

"We had a deal. And you ain't lived up to your end." Dee turns to go.

"Wait, please." Melvin touches Dee's shoulder and Dee turns back, his expression weary. "In a sense, in a sense, Mr. James, Mississippi is a metaphor for all of America. And the wounds here pervade the rest of the country, they're only more visible in the Delta. But then there's also the tremendous bravery. People have risked their lives here for equality, died for the vote."

"People have died here for walking down the damn road. For driving home from the grocery store. What did Cliff die for? His death didn't change nothing. It don't matter if Curtis Roberts is dead or alive, she ain't ever gonna get near the man."

"Let's say that I believe that you don't want Billie to meet Curtis Roberts because you think he is dangerous. But why would Jim McGee not want her to see him?"

"I ain't him."

"Why go to such lengths? I'll tell you what I've come to believe. I think that somehow these men have been involved with what happened to Cliff. But what I haven't puzzled out is why after all this time, you, his brother, would be so resistant. It almost makes it seem as if you might have been involved with what happened to him."

"Man." Dee steps closer. "You better watch what the hell you saying."

Melvin's palms go damp. "Forgive me, but it's one of the few possible explanations I can come up with."

"Shit. Is that what she think? I killed her daddy?"

Melvin wipes his hands on his pants. "I don't know what Billie thinks anymore."

Dee is silent for a moment. "How many stitches?"

"Three on her temple and I believe a few at the back of her head."

"Can't you get her to leave it be? Just let us old men die."

The desperation in Dee's face is hard to look at. "She can't remember what happened, but of course there is a way in which she knows, it's embedded in her muscles, in the way she moves through the world." What a good opening for his chapter on Billie.

"She be fine. Just get her to go back and I'll give you what you want."

"Whatever happened, it's time to let it out."

Dee stubs his cigarette out and flicks it over the railing, walking back into his apartment. The heavy door smacks shut. Melvin turns off the recorder. This isn't quite how he imagined their tête-à-tête would go. He goes to the door and knocks.

"Mr. James? Dee?"

A man sitting down on a chair at the other end of the balcony is staring at him. The door opens. Dee is standing there holding a box.

"I'll give you this on one condition—you don't tell her where you got it."

Melvin nods. "Of course."

Dee closes his eyes for a moment, rubbing his forehead. "You know folks up in Greendale said all kinda things about Cliff when he died. Like he was some Communist brother swaggering round here with an M16 and shit."

"That he was militant?"

Dee looks at him. "Yeah. There was rumors he was part of the Invaders up in Memphis. But he didn't own no black leather jacket."

"Well, he was too old for Vietnam."

"Some folks said he was on drugs. How you gonna claim that when there were none found in his system? Nobody wanted to listen. They said Dee you just a kid. And my mother, my momma said there ain't no justice in this world, baby. We have to wait till the next."

"Billie won't go back until she finds him."

"And what then? Curtis Roberts ain't gonna talk to her and even if he did it'd be nothing but lies. Then all them white trash people are gonna be running her off the road, shooting at her car, and they ain't gonna be too careful. It's too late for any kind of justice. Shit, we should both leave Mississippi, me and her." He nods at the box. "Maybe you can use this to get her to go back east. I can't be involved no more. I'm too goddamned tired." Dee goes back in and shuts the door.

Melvin places the box on the ground and opens it. On top are old issues of the *Chicago Defender*. Cliff's birth and death certificates, his old driver's license. At the bottom are newspaper clippings, a collection of letters of condolence, and finally, the pages.

CHAPTER 1—WHY O WHY

When I moved away from Mississippi, I told myself that I would never return. It was what my mother, Ruby James (née Grant), had wanted, and though she expected that I would visit, she could have never imagined the reasons why I would come back. In 1850, her grandmother, my great-grandmother, Eula, had been born into slavery, and though Eula died long before I was born, my mother never forgot the stories of terror that woman carried, especially the one of being sold off as a young girl in New Orleans. Eula was the root of my mother's family because we had no idea of who our people were before her, before she was forcibly orphaned. But over the years I have come to understand that something more than fear must've been passed down to me from my elders, because not only did Eula experience cruelty and countless other traumas, but she also experienced a radical change: she was freed. Something her mother and her mother's mother, wherever they were, must have been begging God for, but though Eula searched she never found them, and never knew if they lived to see their prayers come true.

My mother and her mother, Mabel, never wanted to talk about slavery days. They were ashamed, I suppose. I was the opposite. I wanted to know all about it, and even as a little boy, I was angry that such an unjust institution had ever been in place. But unlike me, they had seen the mobs, the picnics of hate, felt the daily humiliations that simmer with death. Lynchings were whispered about at night when I was supposed to be asleep.

I had been raised, like most people in my town, to believe that the way things were was the way they were always going to be. White folks had their schools and hospitals and barbershops, and we had ours, or sometimes we didn't. But even if white folks were supposed to be better in every way, I spent most of my time wondering why exactly they had everything and we didn't. Why they could do what they wanted with impunity. Perhaps I would have gone along like a little sheep if I hadn't become such a big reader. Books fired up my imagination and I began dreaming that I was one of the good guys, maybe even the lead hero, who would one day find a way to prosper over the villains that kept us down.

The other part of what was swirling around in me came from my father. William "Willie" James had come home angry from World War II after serving in Japan and China. He hated the way that white soldiers treated him when he was out there fighting for his country, but he spoke in glowing terms of the people he had met in other countries. To them, he was a soldier and a man. When my father first came back from the war, he figured things would be different because *he* was different. He had risked his life, and though he hadn't gone past the seventh grade, he had seen some of the world. The revolution in his spirit did a number on mine. I hung around the porch at night to listen to his cussing about the white "home guards" being formed in the county now that black veterans were coming back. These young black men weren't as militarized as black soldiers would be by the Vietnam War, the army during World War II was still segregated and blacks were mostly assigned to service branches and rarely in combat, but still they had gotten a taste of what it felt like to be out from under Jim Crow.

But when the White Knights rode again and again, dragging mutilated black bodies over the very ground that black families had broken their backs farming, eventually my father could not stand it. He left the South and went to Chicago, leaving my mother and me to fend for ourselves.

As I grew older, the whispers started to take the shape of people I knew. The wild thing is that at the time my best friend was my white neighbor,

Jimmy. Well, Jimmy could hardly believe the stories I'd tell him, or he preferred to believe that those black bodies must've done something bad to earn it. But the world didn't seem to apply to me and Jim, not yet. He never cared that I was colored and I didn't think much about his being white. But when my father was around he didn't like me associating with a white boy. He forbade me to step a foot in Jim's house unless I was helping my mother. I listened to my daddy, fearing the switch, but when he went off to Chicago and took up with another woman, I did as I pleased. Jimmy's mother was a decent, gentle white woman in my estimation who never fussed at us as long as we took off our shoes before coming in the house and didn't terrify the cat.

Of course, now I am positive she knew what was coming because the mother was always the one to do it. Our friendship, the bond between two young boys, had a focus and purity. I wonder if my life since has been a struggle to return to when that life of play and family and God was as natural and entire as the air I breathed.

I can remember the panic I felt as my mother sat me down and told me that I couldn't play with Jimmy no more. That it was the way it was between white and colored folk and I was about to turn thirteen. It broke my heart. But there had been warnings. He could go wherever he wanted in town and I wasn't supposed to go past the railroad tracks.

While he was fishing and reading mystery magazines, my mother had me doing yard work for the white families she cleaned for. She didn't want me picking or chopping cotton, she was adamant about that. But she had done it for Jimmy's family. All of my family had once worked for his family. Not only that, but we lived on their property and they were our landlord. And while I was used to the white kids who took the bus to their school taunting us while we black kids walked, I had begun to notice white men treating me with suspicion. I knew the hushed stories of black folks shot by a passing car of white men, while dancing in a café, while riding on the handlebars of a friend's bike, or being forced to jump off a bridge for no conceivable reason other than the color of their skin, were a reality. But none of this would compare to the awakening that was to come my way.

When I was about fifteen and in high school, the U.S. Supreme Court announced their decision on *Brown v. Board of Education* that all public schools should be integrated. All hell broke loose. It was like White Redemption all over again. My uncle Floyd, who was living then in Vicksburg, signed one of the NAACP's petitions to desegregate the schools and a mob started to gather. The local white paper published all the names, numbers, and home addresses of these black signers. He and his wife both lost their jobs, got a number of death threats, and rocks through their windows. For a while they moved up here to Greendale and I heard about it from my cousins.

A year later, the year after Emmett Till was murdered, I was sweet on a girl I had grown up with named Sheila. She was very beautiful and I have always thought that there was something mystical about her. One Saturday after I had finished working, I walked over to Sheila's house, where she lived with her mother, grandmother, and Uncle Louis.

But as I got closer I saw her kneeling on the side of the road by a car. There was a police car parked behind it. I knew my mother would not want me to take one step closer, but I could not leave Sheila out there crying. Her uncle Louis was lying on the ground, having been shot in the head by Deputy Curtis Roberts. Sheila's hands and arms and dress were soaked with blood. The deputy claimed that Louis was resisting arrest for speeding and had pulled a gun on him. We stood there listening until I told Sheila to get my mother who could drive him to the hospital that took black folk. The deputy watched as we lifted Louis into his own car. He died before we got there. Sheila told me what happened. There was no speeding, no gun, no dispute. I had been fully initiated into an ugly truth: a black man in this country knows there is a chance that he could die violently for no earthly reason and that a good portion of people will say well he must have done something to deserve it.

Curtis Roberts was a vicious white man who

wanted to be important. As far as I was concerned, he thought that being in the Klan or being an officer, which in those days in Mississippi could be the same thing, would make people take notice. There never was a trial, no witnesses came forward. Neither of our mothers would let us make statements. My mother sent me to stay with my father for the summer, and while I was gone she met Dee's father and when I came home he was living with us.

A few years ago, I came back to Mississippi. It was 1969 and Charles Evers had just been elected as the first African American mayor in Mississippi since Reconstruction down in Fayette. I thought that I was coming back as an intellectual, as an artist, to write about Greendale and help care for my mother as she struggled with her health.

But 1969 was also the year after Dr. King had been assassinated and I was lost on the battlefield. I wanted a break from the poetry scene, from the frenzy of sanctimony about how a black poet should be, and I needed to get back to my roots. That first summer back, my daughter came to visit.

Before she was born, I did not know how I would love my child. I never even thought I would have a daughter. I had always imagined myself a father of sons. I did not know, could not know that my love for my child would remove the distance, the skin between me and the world, that I could feel as if all the children in the world were my child, and I would grieve for all unjust sufferings, vicious deaths, ugly indifference. And to call on invisible forces to protect my child was not enough. I needed to understand how the world had created Curtis Roberts and how this had killed Louis Jackson. This book is about me, and this book is about him.

BIG MUDDY

I came back because I had to.
I came back because blood called
and it was my blood already in the ground.

The land called to say: I am your ancestors.
The land called and said: Youngblood, I am the lady
    of the house.

I came back because we did not know
your name   your names   all the names
in the river   in the ground
those who never got to know that
somebody, heirs of their body, would come back
    for them.

Melvin picks up the box and rushes down to his car. Heaven forbid Dee should change his mind. He slips it carefully onto the passenger seat, climbs into the driver's seat, and speeds into the gas station across the street. Parked by the air tank, he dials his partner, leaning on the steering wheel, shaking. The other line picks up.

"This is a very tremendous day in my life."

HOPSEN

ALWAYS HAD THE FEELING SHEILA WAS TOO GOOD FOR HIM. NOT THAT she ever acted that way. When he was young it felt good. He was proud to have won her, to have a queen like that on his arm. But then he started worrying about how she knew the men she did, if they had known her body and that didn't feel so good. He knew she wasn't no virgin when they started dating, but he didn't want any man knowing a part of her he didn't. He wanted to be number one with nobody standing in spots two through ten.

For that reason he didn't like it when Cliff moved back and started coming over all the time like him and Sheila were best friends. He claimed he was writing a book, a history of the adversity that had happened in their town or some bullshit like that. Jerry didn't think much about it at first. Not like he gave a shit about poetry. He was into music. Sheila was the one who had loved English class in high school so he let it go. But then one night he heard her talking to Cliff about her uncle Louis, which had been a real tragedy, talking bout getting some justice against Curtis Roberts. Jerry knew she'd catch hell if any of it went in a book.

She would never have forgiven him. He can't remember another time he wasn't honest with her. He hadn't hardly decided what he was going to do when Curtis Roberts pulled him over one day, made him get out of the car and spread on the side of his car, saying: "Your wife is mixed up with that uppity nigger Cliff James. Spreading lies about me." Curtis hit him in the back of the head with something and Jerry had slid like a sack of potatoes to the mud. Curtis stood over him, saying, "I know you ain't a troublemaker like him, Jerry. I know you know better than that." Then the death threats came, a brick through the front window where his daughter Sandy was watching TV—Marcus wasn't born yet. All over a damn book. He couldn't stand for that. He made certain that he always answered the phone, that Sandy played in the backyard not out front, that they never drove nowhere after dark, and kept his rifle right by his bed. So when they offered him a way out he was bound to take it. To protect his wife and kid. What man would have done different?

He called Cliff from a pay phone at the bus station, told him he wanted to talk and to come to Avalon alone. He didn't know exactly what they were gonna do. Rough him up he supposed. Nothing real bad they said. He would do his part and they could do theirs. It sure as hell didn't bother him if Cliff got a beating after all he got his family caught up in. What was a book by a black man gonna do? Didn't matter if it was talking about one murder or a hundred as long as it was done to a black man. He could bet on that. He'd had it with Cliff, always calling late at night needing to talk to Sheila. Then she'd be tired in the morning, all back talk and burned toast.

He was surprised to find Cliff at Avalon before him. Sitting up near the bar on a stool with a Dixie cup of liquor. The sun was just going and there was a couple arguing in a booth, but nobody else was there, nobody they knew. The Christmas lights above Cliff's head made the ripped walls and the posters glow.

He pulled a stool up to Cliff. "How you doing?"

Cliff turned, maybe already drunk. "What's on your mind, brotherman? I don't have long. I told my daughter I'd put her to bed tonight."

"How much longer she down?"

"Just another week. Trying to make the most of it."

Jerry remembered thinking then that it was good the child was leaving. Wouldn't be safe for her round here while her daddy was making trouble. "I come to talk to you about Sheila." He gestured at the bar for a beer. He'd had one before he left home but he needed another.

"Man, don't be a fool. Whatever you might think is going down between us, it ain't."

That burned him up right there. That Cliff would even assume that was what he was thinking. "I trust my wife not to mess with nobody. I ain't got to worry bout that."

"Then what is it?" Cliff asked but he was looking across the bar, not looking at nothing, not the signed photograph of some big-tittied actress just behind his head so that whenever he moved Jerry could see her big white smile.

"Listen, I know Sheila seen things. Lord knows we all see'd things we'd like to unsee, but you gonna get her killed, or worse, cause there is worse."

"Times are changing, man."

"Not for them it ain't and they gonna do what they think is necessary. As far they concerned, you're up to no good."

"Look, we're Americans too and things don't change unless we fight for it."

"Every black man who ever said that is dead. And as far as I see it, Louis is dead and me and my family ain't gonna die for his dead ass."

Cliff looked at him. "It's up to Sheila what she wants to do, what she's willing to risk."

"You been gone too long to have sense."

"Some of us want to live a life worth living."

"How you talking bout living when you're doing shit that's gonna get you dead? They ain't no Riders or reporters out here no more. The FBI is long gone."

"What you want from me, Jerry? If you want Sheila to stop working with me, talk to her."

"I want you to give up that book."

Cliff laughed. "That's not the way art works."

"Don't say I didn't warn you."

"Oh, I been getting the warnings. But I didn't come back home to play checkers."

Cliff looked at him with what the women liked to call his soulful eyes. Foolishness. But there was something about the way Cliff had looked right then. Old eyes Jerry would have said. Old as the dirt in the unmarked graveyard where his granddaddy could tell him where everyone without a headstone was buried.

"I guess if you don't understand why, then there ain't no words I can tell you." Cliff swung back to the bar.

He had come there to do what he had to. The choice had been Cliff's. Jerry walked outside to where Curtis Roberts and them were waiting in the tilled field behind Avalon. They were sweaty and out of uniform. He could smell the liquor on them. He nodded then went back in.

"Sheila just got here. Waiting outside behind the house to talk to you," he told Cliff. "You can hear from her own mouth how she don't want you to write about Louis."

Cliff looked up at him in disbelief and slammed the empty Dixie cup down. It fell onto its side on the bar and he walked out to where they were waiting to take him.

BILLIE

IT IS HER BIRTHDAY. SHE IS THIRTY-FIVE, THREE YEARS OLDER THAN her father when he died. She used to worry that she would not make it to thirty-two, that some freak accident would happen, that she would be hit by a car as she crossed the street or an anvil would fall on her head. But she has lived on with the forehead creases and plucked gray hairs to prove it.

The worst part of her mother's death was waiting for her to die. Those two weeks between morphine and starvation and pain. No more food they said, nothing to prolong the body. It will be quick they said, but it wasn't.

She doesn't know what she's waiting for. The rain to be over, a call about her vandalized house, the fear to die down. Sometimes she is still waiting for her mother not to be dead.

It's a mistake to leave the motel. But she can't stand another minute in the dark room, which smells like bleach and the last fifty occupants. She walks along the highway toward the glare of the Dollar General, the gun in her bag slapping against her leg.

He is out of context, standing in the narrow laundry detergent aisle with a little boy at his side. When he turns, he stares at her busted lip, the remains of her black eye. Under the store's fluorescent lights her bruises look green. They stop in front of each other at the dryer sheets. The little boy follows, sandy haired and blue eyed. He too is fascinated by her lopsided face.

"Hi," Harlan says. "Tyler, this is Miss Billie, she lives down the road from your granddaddy. This is my son, Tyler."

"What happened to her face?" Tyler asks.

"Sorry," Harlan says and bends, turning the boy toward him. "Buddy, we don't ask those kind of questions, it's not polite."

"It's okay," she says. But she doesn't know what to tell the kid. He must be five or six, probably too young to say she got into a fight. It's too dumb to say she fell.

"Why don't you go get that bouncy ball you saw, okay?"

The boy skitters away happy and Harlan straightens. Outside, rain starts to sweep across the road. "What happened?"

"I got into a fight."

"I can see that."

"I guess the gods were with them."

"Who attacked you?"

She checks in the aisle behind him for signs of the kid. "Two guys."

"What in the hell? Where at?"

"The dog park, weirdly enough. They must have been

following me." The candy bar in her hand is starting to melt, the chocolate slipping inside of the wrapper.

"Following you?" He drops his voice; he's the one looking behind him now. "They do anything else?"

She looks at the dryer sheets. "No. But they shot Rufus."

"Are you kidding me? That's crazy." He runs a hand over his mouth. "Want me to come over and sleep in the living room?"

"No. Thanks. I wouldn't want to get you involved in whatever this is." And she doesn't know to what degree his family may already be involved. It's not that she blames Harlan. It really doesn't seem like he knows anything. But he certainly wouldn't choose her over his family.

"Did you know them? What did the police say?"

"I can't talk about it here. Your son is coming."

The little boy pulls at Harlan's jeans, clutching a purple ball to his chest. "Daddy, look."

"That's a good one, honey," Harlan says without looking.

She walks back to the motel in the rain. Everything is fine except when she gets there she's not home and can't hear the rain dripping off the trees. She makes a new pot of coffee, drinking cup after cup until her head hurts. Her cell phone rings. It's him. Somewhere in this town he is waiting for her to pick up. So much of her life she has gone without. Can't she have this if only for a minute? Who needs to know but her and him?

An hour later, she unlocks the door and steps out. It's cloudy and a few birds are singing in the sad trees around the world's saddest swimming pool next to the parking lot. She watches him take the spiral steps two at a time.

"It's my birthday," she says as he picks her up.

When burning hot, the coffee doesn't taste too bad. They share a cup sitting on the bed. In lieu of cake, he gets her M&M's from the vending machine. When she brings him a paper cup of water from the sink, he takes her hand.

"I'm sorry somebody hurt you. I hate it."

"It's not your fault," she says.

"I know, but I can still care."

She doesn't know why but that it is right to kneel on the carpet and rest her head in his lap. He puts the water on the bedside table so that he can stroke her hair. She doesn't know how much time has passed when he helps her climb on his lap and wrap her legs round his waist, thumbs through the loops of her jeans, and presses his mouth to hers.

He has holes in the toes of his socks and freckles over his shoulders. They laugh at this as they undress. If only she were wearing more exciting underwear, but nothing else was clean. She strips back the comforter and he lies back on white sheets raw with bleach. She sits on top of him because of her ribs.

"You're beautiful," he says.

Only the bathroom light is on and what sunlight escapes the curtains makes the outline of the window glow. Hopefully the shadows hide her bruises, the ones on her waist that other hands gave and the sick yellow down her legs and back. He is gentle because he has to be. They are careful, but this is reckless. If only she could be inside this moment for a hundred years where they are nobody but them.

For her birthday, he drives her to visit Rufus. They scratch under his ears and stroke his nose. They tell him at the same time that he is a good boy. They both get wet eyes but don't cry. What is it about a sweet dog? She will not let herself cry when Harlan leaves, but then he doesn't.

TWO WEEKS LATER, HE SAYS IT GETS EVEN HOTTER, HEAVIER BY JULY. They sit on the porch in the drowsy afternoon listening to invisible four-wheelers whine somewhere across the fields. The air gleams on their skin as the shadows of the trees billow over the grass. Rufus is in the living room with a fan pointed at him as he sleeps on his new dog bed. She leans on Harlan, putting her nose to his shoulder, smelling him. It's not that he says he will protect her. It's laughable that she's living with a man who says that. A man who takes her swimming in a creek he promises doesn't have too many snakes. A man who fixes her bike and the leaky faucet. A man who has his gun on while she wears hers. Please let this be a clearheaded fever.

That afternoon, in the makeup aisle looking at foundation for the purple ring around her eye, Billie smiles when she catches Harlan carrying a six-pack and carton of ice cream. Not ready to join him at the register, she waves him off and goes down the medicine aisle, searching for antibiotic ointment.

"Fancy date," Lacey says. Her hair has been dyed brown but left blond on the top. She wears it in a low bun coming loose.

"We drove all the way down here to avoid anyone we know and here you are."

"He do that?" Lacey nods at her eye.

"Of course not." Behind her back, Billie slips the foundation on the cold-medicine shelf.

"Use concealer too. You need to brighten it first."

Lacey walks off wearing a yellow and black varsity-style jacket, but in place of a letter is a big yellow weed leaf. When Billie goes to the front of the store, she doesn't see either of them. But outside Lacey is waiting, slamming a bottle of chocolate milk into the palm of her hand like a pack of cigarettes.

"Your uncle's looking for you." Lacey twists off the top and drinks.

"Your hair looks nice dark." But she should have dyed it all the way.

"He's real worried about you."

Billie puts on her sunglasses. "I'll call him when I'm ready."

"Hey, I'm the last person to get caught up in other people's shit, but you are taking your sweet time." Lacey lights a cigarette. "I'm trying to be nice."

"Then be nice to my uncle and don't say anything."

Lacey's big sneakers make her legs look even thinner. "I don't lie to Dee," she says.

"Fine, tell my uncle you saw me, but leave out that you saw him."

"You ought not get mixed up with that family." Lacey finishes the milk and throws it in the trash.

"It's between him and me, not them."

Lacey looks at her. "I could slap you silly."

Harlan pulls his truck up to the entrance. The window comes down and he nods to Lacey, then says to Billie, "Ready?" His hair curls up beautifully, terribly from under his hat.

"Yeah." Billie's face flushes down her neck.

Lacey flicks the ash from her cigarette. "You remember me?" she says to Harlan.

He nods. "You're one of Debbi's friends."

"Used to be. But she's what my mama calls a bad penny."

The only fight Billie got in at school was with a girl who shoved her against the sink in the smokers' bathroom. At fifteen, the girl had tattoos and there were rumors that she'd had two abortions and been in a gang. There was a creamy brightness to her, made starker by the dark lipstick. You think you're cute, the girl said. Afterward, when Billie saw her in the hall, it was like they were searching for each other. The girl knew about the world in ways Billie only suspected. But then her mother moved them again.

As the truck pulls away, Harlan says, "So you do know her."

"Not as well as you, I imagine."

"I don't know her at all!"

Billie looks out her window. "She's seeing my uncle."

"Then why did you lie about it?"

"I didn't know if I could trust you."

He brakes at the stoplight and looks at her. "And now?"

"Everything is different now." She reaches over and takes off his hat, running her unbroken hand through his hair.

JIM MCGEE

HE DIDN'T KNOW THEN WHY HE THOUGHT OF HER AFTER CHARLOTTE was born, staring at his baby girl through the nursery glass. But in retrospect it seems appropriate. His fine old dad had sped his Plymouth straight from the country club where he had been meeting up with some committee buddies. He arrived still in his golf clothes and stood next to Jim, eyes straining behind his glasses to find the tiny infant under all those tubes and wires. His mother had left her bridge club or some such thing and brought Marlene's hospital bag stuffed with nightgowns and Pond's cold cream, which in their rush to get Harlan squared away with his sister-in-law, he and Marlene had forgotten at home. His father was not an affectionate man, but in front of the nursery he put an arm around Jim's shoulders. Jim thought about toy soldiers, lightning bugs, begging for ice cream from the icebox.

At the hospital, Marlene almost never spoke, lighting up

only when they brought Harlan to visit. Gone was her talk of Charlotte being a sweet little majorette or growing up a Cotton Queen like Marlene had been, organizing luncheons and charity events. Marlene thought it important that a woman be civic-minded.

He had thought this kind of thing happened to his grandfather's generation or great-grandfather's when the Delta was still being carved out from the swamp and brush and people died from infected wounds and a whole host of fevers, when you were lucky if out of ten kids you kept six. He'd never understood how any parent lived through the death of their child, and yet here he was living out the unimaginable.

Later, his mother came to the nursery carrying Harlan, who had cut-up knees from falling in the playhouse that his father had built. His father was so gentle with his grandson. Not at all like he'd been with him. Harlan adored his Poppaw.

"Is that her, Daddy?" Harlan reached for him and Jim took the boy in his arms, noticing that he was wearing something different from when they had dropped him off that morning.

"Yes, Bubba, that's Charlotte."

"Is she sick?"

He wanted to lie, but he shouldn't because the baby was dying. If he just didn't think that word *dying,* he could get through it.

"A little bit, honey. She came kinda early and is having trouble with her breathing."

"Her lungs Grandma said." Harlan looked at him in sad triumph.

"That's right."

A life in three days. What could that life know? What did he want her to know? Warmth? Safety? Soft voices? Could she feel she was loved in that space of time so soon from the cave of the womb? God's plan. God's plan.

Then Harlan laid his head on his shoulder, and Jim got a flash of Billie, who had done the same when he rocked her in the spare room. Was that it? Was it a part of God's plan to show him what it felt like to have a daughter taken away?

Jim isn't surprised by the fact of Dee calling him, but by the sound of his voice on the phone. A voice worn with cigarettes and resentment. Cliff used to like to hear his little brother sing. Thought he had the better voice. Mailed him records all the time. The Four Tops, James Brown.

"I ain't want to call, but felt I had to."

Jim sits down with the cordless. He spills Diet Coke on the couch and stands up. Nowhere can be comfortable when he is scattered between decades like this.

"What's on your mind?"

"You seen my niece." It is not a question.

"Yes, she's come by." The ceiling is suddenly too low, or maybe he's always found it that way. He's retired, he could remodel.

"What you tell her?"

"Nothing to tell."

"I've done the best I could to keep her clear of the business, but I can't do no more."

"What do you want me to do about it?"

"Let her see him," Dee says.

"That dog won't hunt."

"Them Robertses found her and attacked her. My niece. Cliff's daughter. I can't have none of that, Jimmy."

"How's telling her where he's at gonna solve it?"

"You make her understand that you'll tell her on condition that she leave. Let her do her thing, then she'll go."

"Why d'you think I know where he is?"

"White folk always know where the devil be at."

Maybe Dee has been waiting to say that to him. "I'll tell you again it sounds like a bad idea."

"Listen up, till now I ain't done nothing. I've kept my head down and mouth shut. So if I'm finally gonna do one thing it's got to be right."

"Why should I get myself involved in this damn mess?"

Dee laughs softly. "Oh Jimmy, Jimmy. You involved in more ways than you know. Your son is with her."

Jim sits back down. "What do you mean?"

"They's living together at the house. Better talk to him before your wife find out. I've got to get Billie out of this town, and I know in my heart that this is the only way she will go."

Jimmy was something only Cliff called him. His parents called him James, his friends called him Jim. Dee had picked it up as a kid. He had known this moment would come. He didn't know how it would but that it would. But he never dreamed that Harlan would be involved. That twist seems like a divine trick.

His son has never quite turned out the way he had hoped. Wasn't interested in farming, but then neither had he been. Didn't last a full year at Ole Miss. He was thirty-one now and didn't have much of a career and still hung round with a bunch of idiots. But then the boy he'd brought into the world was a joy to be around. He was kind and did the best he could by people. His own father had been a good man but limited. A churchgoing man who liked being somebody in the community and hoped that Jim would go to law school and run for office, not become an accountant.

Marlene wanted Harlan to be a quintessential southern gentleman, genteel in khakis with a wife in silk, sons in bow ties and little daughters in bows. To go to Ole Miss then Harvard Business School and be on all the right boards of directors like her daddy. But Harlan dropped out of high school and a few years later got stuck with a girl who was rough around the edges, as Jim chose to say. Marlene liked to say a lot worse. As long as Jim had known Debbi's family they were poor and had stayed poor. She wasn't a bad girl, she just was so used to ugly behavior that she didn't know better. No softness in her life. Maybe Marlene was placing her hopes in Tyler by taking him to Boy Scouts and Sunday school every week.

He calls Harlan to him, who leaves the girl and her dog to fend for themselves in what must be a haunted house. But when he sees his light-headed son, his heart sinks. The boy thinks he's in love.

Harlan sits while he stands, placing himself in front of the fireplace as he usually does. Where he has held forth on the birds and the bees, the decision to sell off a good chunk of farmland, and countless speeches about Debbi. "Son, none of us know what God has planned for us. But we do the best we can. Nothing about what I'm gonna say is exactly fair, but I sincerely hope that you have enough faith in me to know I have tried to do what I thought was best."

"Dad, you're kind of freaking me out."

Jim smiles. "I'm taking my time cause it's not an easy thing to say." He leans a hand on the mantel. "I know you're staying at the house with Billie."

Harlan looks around. "Is Mom home?"

"Not yet. I haven't told her."

Harlan's eyes meet his. "All right. And it makes you uncomfortable?"

"I knew her daddy, knew him real well. We were very close when we were kids. And while she's been here, I've tried to look out for her on behalf of her father."

Harlan pushes his hair back from his face. It's getting too long. "You heard she got beat up then?"

"Maybe I haven't done too good of a job. I just figured people had moved on, that it would stay in the past."

"You mean her daddy's accident?"

"Son, let me finish. She's been looking for a man, the last man to see her father alive, and that man don't want to be found. But I know where he's at."

Harlan looks at him. "Was it an accident, Dad?"

"I couldn't say." And he can't, not to his son. "It's no good her being here. Those men who attacked her? They ain't gonna leave her alone. They'll harass her the minute you turn your back and even when you don't. Their kin knows the sheriff and he's not going to lift a finger against them. The time for any sort of justice for Cliff has passed, if it ever came." The clock is too loud in the room. He should

THE GONE DEAD 263

move it to the garage. He's never liked hearing time hacked away. "I will tell her where he lives. But then I need you to keep your distance."

"You think I would let her go to see this crazy old guy alone?"

"She has family that will go with her. Or that academic she's hanging around with."

"Forget it, Dad. I'm going with her."

"Harlan, I want you to think about what's best for you and Tyler. You don't need another thing on your record. And you know the sheriff is no friend of ours, so don't go offering yourself up on a platter." He puts a hand up. "I know, I know you want to rush out and save her, but Billie doesn't belong here. We need to do the thing that will allow her to go."

"Dad." Harlan sighs. "I don't want her to get hurt any more."

"Neither do I. Trust me on this, this is the best way."

HARLAN

HE HASN'T ASKED HIMSELF IF IT COULD BE SERIOUS. HE WASN'T IN A rush to know. Whatever it is she feels it's the same for him, even if she never says it and never will.

Sure on the surface, they got almost nothing in common. He can't picture her happy drinking beer at a crawfish boil after church on Sunday. (Would they even go to the same church?) And he can't picture himself living in a cramped city riding the subway with a million other people where he can't fish or ride his motorcycle. Imagine his mother passing on the family silver to a girl who doesn't even like to garden.

When he pulls up to the house, Billie is out front with a few purple coneflowers in one hand and a fifth of whiskey in the other. She looks pretty even with the yellow shadows of old bruises. He could wait. They could drive down to New Orleans, get a room in a fancy hotel in the Quarter, live it up for a few nights.

As he climbs out of the truck, the sky dims as if it were getting on for night and not just cloudy. *Love* is a word people overuse anyway. He sees her and she sees him. And it don't matter if she never sees Curtis Roberts. An old backwoods Klansman like Curtis ain't gonna start spilling his heart out to her.

She waves then walks up to the truck. "What's wrong?" she asks as he gets out.

"Nothing. Just hungry."

"Don't know if I can help you with that."

He puts his arms around her and kisses her neck. He's not ready. Inside, he begins to make rice and beans using the only pot she has. He hears her come in to check on Rufus. She's a dedicated but pretty jumpy nurse.

At the stove, she slips her arms around his waist and presses up against him from behind. "What is it?" she says.

He leads her by the hand into the bedroom. "Sit down."

She stops smiling when she sees his face. "Whatever it is just hurry up and tell me."

"I saw my father this afternoon."

"Okay." She is studying him for clues. "And he's not happy about us, right?"

"Not particularly, but it's not that."

She shimmies back on the air mattress so that she is leaning against the chipped wall.

"Our families . . ." Everything seems too still in the dim room. Like the stacks of books and pile of dirty laundry have sat here forever.

"Are we related?"

He looks up at her. "What? Hell no."

"I just wondered. Since your dad sold my grandmother the house, I wondered if maybe over the years there'd been some relations."

"He didn't say anything of the kind, thank god." He stands and pulls open the blinds he's just put up. He stays at the window, looking out at his truck. "My father can give you Curtis Roberts's address." She's quiet and he turns to her.

She covers her face. "I'm not ready—shit, how do I get ready?"

"Well, don't go alone. It won't be safe."

She jumps up and starts pulling on her boots.

"I better check if the water's boiling."

"Wait," she says.

He stops in the doorway.

"Is this it?" she asks.

He leans in the doorway, not looking her in the eye. "We both know that this was never gonna work out in the long term."

"So you're not coming with me?"

"You're gonna go and question him and that's your right."

Her face flushes. "Are you implying that it's not important that I do?"

"Billie, I gotta be honest with you, he's not going to tell you a thing."

"I have to confront him. And, I can't believe I'm having to say this to you, but the fact that no one has wanted me to find him is huge."

"It don't mean that he killed your daddy."

After she finishes pulling on her boots, she walks up to him until she's a few inches away. "You mean that your father wasn't involved in his death."

"He wasn't. He loved your family."

"We were black."

"Don't play the race card with me."

She tilts her face, eyes wide. "Are you going to say next that you didn't own any slaves your ancestors did, and *the* blacks are racist against you all the time?"

He tries to take her by the shoulders but she steps back. "I don't want to talk like this with you," he says.

He grabs her hand and she lets him hold it for a minute, then pulls away.

"Whether you get what you're looking for or not, you'll leave. I live here."

"You don't have to," she says, folding her arms over her chest.

He shakes his head. "This is home. That's what you don't understand."

She doesn't say anything and he doesn't look back as he gets in his truck and leaves.

BILLIE

IN SCANDINAVIA, PEOPLE ESCAPED FROM BERGEN AND BUILT A VIL-
lage in Tusededal, where the plague found them and killed
them all except for one eight-year-old girl. When she was
found, she had become practically feral so they named her
Rype, wild bird. Another little girl in another little town
was locked in the storeroom by her father. The whole village
died of the plague, but she lived on alone, waiting to be freed
by strangers.

Her phone rings. Carlotta, Dr. Hurley, Uncle Dee, Jude.
The only person she answers is Jim McGee. What he gives
her is not so much an address as it is directions to a loca-
tion. A place in the woods where the devil waits. He'll know
where it is if she disappears. Apparently, he always does.

"I'm sorry," he says.

What kind of sorry is he? Does he want her to forgive him?

"You were at my house when you went missing."

"For how many hours?" she says.

"For two days."

And all she thinks she knew curls up and burns away.

"Two days?" Her brain scrambles to make new pictures.

"I don't know what you knew. We told you he was dead and that your mother was coming to get you. And then she did."

Mom knew. This whole time. "Why didn't she tell me?"

"Why would she want to tell you something horrible like that? It happened when you were a little girl. And we kept you safe with us until she came."

"You don't know what I was thinking. Or what happened before you got me."

"No, I don't. Though neither do you."

"But I am her, I am that Billie too."

After the call, she curls up on the floor next to Rufus and strokes his nose. Splinters sway in the dust under the turn of the fan. It's terrible to have to leave him here alone. Harlan would probably adopt him if anything happens. There's a knock at the door. Rufus tries to get up and howls.

THEY PASS THROUGH SMALL TOWNS WITH GAS STATIONS AND COLD beer ads and kudzu that threatens to bury the street signs. They pass old cars and dilapidated houses, bare-chested kids cruising by on bikes. She has never gone this way or driven down this dirt road into the woods, which seems private but there is nothing marking it as such. Dr. Hurley tells them about the murder of Louis Jackson and her father's book. Billie is silent, feeling the gun against her stomach.

When they arrive, the white trailer looks tilted, as if it has been sinking slowly over the years headfirst into the mud. The porch is filled with a collection of random chairs and different-size coolers, but there's an order to their arrangement. The trees surrounding the trailer are coated in sunlight and behind them wisteria blooms and its petals decorate the ground. Even here in the dragon's lair there is beauty.

Carlotta knocks on the door. There is movement inside and someone heavy approaches. Dread is on her tongue, hard in her belly, around the knot at the back of her throat.

Curtis Roberts is wearing a worn but clean plaid shirt, jeans, and an Ole Miss ball cap. He is a mountain of a man, his red face almost too small for his body. Tattoos on the underside of each forearm. He has a salt-and-pepper beard, neatly trimmed. Some of the hair on his head is so dark that it looks dyed. He has a tight jaw, perhaps an underbite. If she passed him on the street she would think he looked poor, harmless.

Dr. Hurley speaks first. "Hello, Mr. Roberts? I'm a professor from a university in North Carolina and I'm working on a book about a poet named Clifton James who lived here in Greendale and I'm wondering if you would have some time to talk to us about him?"

Curtis peers at each of their faces. "Who? Don't know who you mean."

"When you were a deputy in 1972, you found Cliff James's body near one of the tenant homes on the McGees' farm. You do remember Jim McGee, don't you? He was there too."

"Was he a black guy?"

"Yes, Cliff was. Do you remember finding his body? You were an officer on duty when he died."

"I remember, but it's been a minute. I don't have long to talk. I was just about to go out."

"We'll make it as quick and painless as possible," Dr. Hurley says at his most jovial. "May we sit?"

Curtis is wearing worn loafers with no socks, sort of unofficial house slippers. She can't imagine him young, can't imagine him thirty years ago. They sit down on the chairs scattered along the porch. Billie is the last to join, choosing a red cooler as her seat.

"Did you know Cliff before that night?" Carlotta asks, her voice low, face rigid.

"No. I mean, I think I'd seen him around, but I didn't know him." His hands are bulky, almost swollen, perhaps arthritic.

Dr. Hurley leans forward. "And do you remember finding anything about his death suspicious?"

"He fell and hit his head, right?"

"That is what the police report tells us."

"If I'm not badly mistaken, he'd been drinking," Curtis says. Around them the rattle of locusts rises. "That's all I know about it. Like I said, I gotta get going."

"I'm his daughter," Billie says.

They all look at her. No more waiting. Curtis nods with large eyes. He has a hunted look.

Billie turns to Dr. Hurley and Carlotta. "Could you leave us alone for a minute? Please." They look like they want to resist but she turns to Curtis. "Can I talk to you inside? It'll be quick."

"Okay," he says and she is surprised by how easily he agrees, as if he too has been waiting all his life. What a relief to find the one place where they are the same.

CARLOTTA

"WE CAN'T LEAVE HER IN THERE WITH HIM." DR. HURLEY'S EYES ARE so big they're about to pop out of his head.

The woods around the trailer are quiet enough so that they can hear the murmur of the two voices. "Why not," she says without taking her eyes away from the door.

He paces the porch. "You know she's got a gun."

"So does he, somewhere in that dump."

"She could do—she could hurt him."

The wind comes through the trees like it's rushing to see what's going on. "Dr. Melvin, ain't nothing stopping you from going in there."

He puts a hand on her shoulder. "But certainly there are other ways to get justice, wouldn't you agree? Even if he is a murderer."

Still she will not be moved. "I been waiting for over thirty years and it ain't here yet."

"This is not the way it's supposed to be. I can't— What about as a Christian?"

"'But if thou do that which is evil, be afraid; for he beareth not the sword in vain: for he is the minister of God, a revenger to execute wrath upon him that doeth evil.'"

"But does not Romans also say: 'Dearly beloved, avenge not yourselves, but rather give place unto wrath: for it is written, Vengeance is mine; I will repay, saith the Lord.'"

Carlotta nods. "Uh-huhn, all right. This is the way I see it, this is the moment that God ordained. He sent Cliff's child here to reckon with that fallen man. I always thought I'd be the one to finally confront him, but no, this is the way. And I ain't gonna interfere with His wrath or His mercy."

He throws up his hands. "This is madness. If Billie hurts him, she is the one who will go to jail, not him."

"I'm not gonna tell nobody, are you?"

He doesn't answer and she smiles.

BILLIE

INSIDE, SHE SITS ON A FOLDING CHAIR WHILE HE SITS ON THE COUCH, hunched over his own lap. The trailer is too small for him.

"I'm his daughter."

"I know, you said."

He looks sick. Or does she just think he looks sick, want him to look sick, eaten up by whatever he did.

"All I want . . . you could tell me what happened to my father, you could."

"Far as I know he had an accident and hit his head."

She is silent. There must be something she could say to make him implicate himself. "You didn't get along, did you?"

"Didn't know him good enough to get along or not. I ain't done nothing to him if that's what you think."

"I know about Louis Jackson. That you shot him."

He looks at her, then back down. "That there was self-defense, justifiable homicide. It's been proven in a court of law. I don't need to comment on that now."

The air-conditioning is sticking to her skin. "Were you in the Klan?"

"No."

"Come on. What about when you were young?"

"I went to a meeting or two when I was young cause I was curious. At that time a lot of folks did. But I knew very little about their goings-on. My daddy wouldn't have liked it." His eyes are wide, as if that is what innocence looks like.

"Did you have friends in the Klan?"

"Some of them were, some of them weren't."

"Did any of them have something against my father because he was involved with civil rights?"

"I ain't know nothing about that. I know people didn't like strangers coming down to judge us. Who would? Some in the Klan weren't even against blacks and whites being together, no matter what you might hear. They wanted it to happen gradual and not be forced on them by the federal government."

"Why did you go to the meetings? Did it give you a sense of purpose?" She sits a little forward so that she can move her hand under her loose T-shirt and feel where the gun is. "That's what I've always thought about the Klan."

"It was just what— My uncle went, other folks I knew, so I went once or twice too. Like I said."

"My father was writing a book about you and Louis Jackson. I know that now. But what I want to know is what you did about it."

"Folks can write whatever they want about me. I got nothing to hide."

This is getting her nowhere. He's not going to confess. She shifts back, looking around the trailer. A woman's shirt is hanging off the back of the couch, pink sandals by the door. Pictures on the wall near the kitchenette of Curtis holding a baby in a diaper. Grandkids.

Her eyes are hot. "Are you married?" She had been picturing him alone, full of the deed that had rotted his whole life.

"Yeah, my wife just went out to the store."

She blinks the tears back. "Your wife. Why do you get to have a wife while my daddy lies dead in the ground?" She stands up, slipping her hand back under her shirt. "You know I can't really remember him? I have these little freeze-frames and that's it. I can't feel what he was like."

"It's got nothing to do with me."

She takes out the gun. He jumps up, his hands pushing toward her. "What are you doing?"

She swings the gun at him. "Stop moving. Sit back down." She steps closer. "Sit."

He sits. "You don't want to use that, not a girl like you."

"You know what I'll say? I'll say self-defense. Like you with Louis Jackson." She walks backward to the door and gropes for the lock, turning it. "There. Now it's just me and you." A line of sweat drips down her outstretched arm.

"I go to church now."

"That's interesting. Does the thought of hell bother you? Especially now that you're older, closer to death." She steps over an ashtray, moving slowly where the floor dips, until she's a couple of feet away. "There. See, now I can't miss."

"You want to be a murderer?"

"Just tell me what happened that night and I'll go. It's easy. Just do it."

"I told you I wasn't involved!" He almost gets up.

"Sit down." Her hands are shaking the gun.

"I wasn't the one!"

"What do you mean?"

"I wasn't the one. I swear!"

"You tell me." She steps closer until the barrel presses into the side of his forehead. It feels so good her heart might jump from her chest.

Curtis's breathing goes ragged. "You ain't got it right. I wanted to scare him off, teach him a lesson. I don't hardly know. We waited for him outside of some juke joint and gave him a whupping. That's it."

"Then what?"

He wrings his hands over and over in his lap. "Well, I reckon he was pretty bad off. A few hours later we got a call that he had died, so we come over as officers. It was a terrible thing. You was there. We didn't know at first. You were crying. You heard everything." His eyes dart up at her. "You was that little girl."

"Yes." She remembers to breathe. "Then what happened? Did I go missing?"

"One of the deputies took you. He quit not long after that. He never was no good at it. Jim McGee, he took you home with him. Thought we were gonna hurt you, I reckon."

"Were you?"

"No, ma'am. I would never harm a child."

"But you did."

Someone starts beating on the door. He looks but she doesn't.

"Now I told you all I know. I can't tell you nothing more. I told you it was an accident."

"You know what I would like?" she says. The door shudders.

"Billie!" Her uncle's voice.

But everyone else is in another time and place; only they are near to each other.

"I would like my mother. And I would like my father. I would like a mom and a dad. That would feel good. They were good people. They fought on behalf of other people. They probably even understood the forces that created someone like you."

"Billie, open this door!"

"But me, I'm not good as them. And I can't ever have what I want."

"Billie." Her uncle sounds underwater. "Let me tell you everything. I know all kind of stuff he don't. Don't you go and do something we all will regret."

She looks at Curtis Roberts. "Are you right with the Lord? Isn't that what they say?"

"Listen, listen I got kids, a wife . . ."

"Billie"—her uncle slaps the door—"your daddy would not want this. I promise you it would break his heart. I promise you."

She swallows. "Go home, Uncle Dee. This is just me. Nothing to do with you."

"Your daddy believed in forgiveness."

"What about justice?" The arm holding the gun is beginning to burn.

"He was a man of God."

She looks at Curtis. "He's not sorry."

"I am!" says Curtis.

"You're sorry you did it? Or sorry I'm making you feel scared? Whatever you are it's not enough. Not for me."

"Let me help you get justice, Billie," her uncle says. "He did it, but he ain't know all the truth. I know, I can help you. We can get it, you and me."

"How do you know?"

"Because it's been long time coming. Don't you want to be free? Free of that weight you been carrying? Open the door."

Curtis's eyes are fixed on her. Right now she is everything to him. But which way to freedom. It cannot be undone if she does it. In one second it would be over and just begun. He would be out of this world and she would have done it. And would Mom and Daddy ever have thought that their footnote of a daughter would end up a local news story for shooting a man dead? She pulls the trigger. Curtis yells and drops to the floor, shaking. The bullet has buried itself in the wall on his left.

"Now you know what it feels like when someone wants you dead."

She opens the door. Her uncle grabs her and pulls her away, almost off her feet. She doesn't know where the gun goes or how long it is before she's wrapped in the stinging heat of her uncle's car.

Her uncle is standing above her shouting, "Why y'all just gonna sit here and have her ruin her life? He would never forgive me—never!" He ducks down and presses his forehead to hers. "It's all right, Billie, it's all right, we'll get you back to Philadelphia, we'll tell all the newspapers, and the senators, and—"

"No. I have to stay. I have to see it through, you and me, right? You and me."

It's all right, Billie, her daddy always said. He would sit her down in the living room and put the TV on. When the door closed behind him, she thought he would come back. Sometimes he left her but he always came back.

DEE

HE WAS TURNING EIGHTEEN THAT YEAR. WHEN THEY HEARD THE CAR horn outside, his mother looked out the window and told him to go and take Billie out to his brother's car. His niece was curled up asleep on the couch.

He got to the car and saw his brother in the driver's seat. Dee had never seen him looking like that. Cliff was smoking a cigarette but his hands were shaking and he was bleeding everywhere—his eyebrow, mouth, from his ear—but he didn't want to go to the hospital he said. Don't tell Momma, Cliff said. He was his big brother. Dee lay Billie on the back-seat.

Dee guessed right away that some white men did it. Other folk said things had changed, and they had some, but some things hadn't. He never thought too much about it. But Cliff did. Cliff was always going on about Hiram Revels and the massacre at Fort Pillow. How even when Dee went to high school with whites and blacks, everything else was still separate—where he sat during lunch, church, Little League, homecoming. Dee didn't care about if he could vote because as far as he was concerned the vote was between having nothing or having even less. He didn't do all that well in school and nobody but Cliff—not his teachers, not his friends—expected more from him. Ever since he'd been back, Cliff came over for his exams and book reports and helped him write his college application. He was supposed to be going in the fall. He wasn't sure he wanted to go, but Cliff said he had to at least give it a chance.

He said nothing to his mother, and after she went to sleep, he went over late that night to check on Cliff.

The house was dark. Not even the porch light on. When he walked up, he could not see. He knocked gently at first, not wanting to wake up his little niece, but there was no answer and he knocked harder. Then he tried the door and it was unlocked. In the hall, he turned on a light. He wanted to check that Cliff was all right, convince him to go up to the hospital, fuck whatever he said.

But Cliff wasn't in his room. Dee called and called his name. Then he remembered his niece and went to the back hallway where she slept but she wasn't in her bed. He really started to panic and hollered for her. But nobody answered.

He went back out in the yard and double-checked that Cliff's car was there. He called for them both, but nothing. Then from the light coming through the living room window, he saw the outline of a hand in the grass. It was his brother lying facedown, collapsed, but still breathing a little.

When he called the police, an ambulance didn't come.

Only two patrol cars and two men, Oakes and Roberts. Not in uniform but in their shirtsleeves. Roberts acting like they done pulled him out of a bar. They handcuffed Cliff as he lay there and Dee started screaming, trying to pull them off his brother. But they wrestled him away, then Oakes checked Cliff's pulse, saying he's dead anyway and all the life flew out of Dee's body.

They made a call and grabbed Dee again, talking like he might have done something to his brother, questioning him over and over. He was wearing a new shirt. It had blood on it now. There was blood under his fingernails too. Cliff's blood, which was his blood, half his blood. He didn't want them touching Cliff's body. He wanted them to leave Cliff as he was. Only his mother should touch him or someone that loved him.

When they let him go, he lit a cigarette to get rid of the smell. It couldn't be the body because it was too soon. Wasn't it too soon? But there was a smell that was bothering him. Maybe it wasn't the body but the smell of somebody's cigar. Somebody smoking a cigar. What did they care? Just another black man dead.

As the sun was starting to rise, Jimmy McGee pulled up. He looked at Dee and gave him a sad nod but nothing else, trying to be professional. He went right to Cliff's body, which was all he was now. Then Jimmy went over to the other men, who left Dee to talk in a little huddle. The side of his jaw was hurting like he might have a bad tooth.

Dee got up and went in the house, calling for Billie again and something moved on Cliff's unmade bed. A bump under the blankets.

"Billie?" There was no answer.

He pulled at the quilt. There she was with her eyes wide open. "Why you hiding?" He picked her up. "Were you asleep?"

"The men were shouting."

"I know, honey."

"Daddy said don't come outside."

What had the baby seen? He didn't know but she knew and would never know.

"It's all right now," he said, smoothing her hair back from her face.

He found some candy in the kitchen. The dirty dishes in the sink were collecting flies. He sat her in the living room and put on the TV, looking for something she could watch.

"I want *Sesame Street*," she said.

"No, baby, that's only on in the morning. It's too late."

He chose some late-night show but she only watched him. The bottoms of her feet were dirty, there was grass on the bottom of her nightdress.

"I'm hungry. I want pasta," she said. "Make the men go away."

"I get you something in a minute. You wait here for me."

"Daddy doesn't like it."

"What don't he like?"

She looked at the front door. "The moon."

He didn't think things could get worse, but then it all began to get real out of hand. Outside, they wanted him to come down to the station, said they'd talk to his momma. He felt scared but he was also watching himself at a distance, wondering if he was feeling like he should feel, like a man should, his brother being dead, his big brother, Cliff. Cliff. Oakes and Roberts went into the house and tried talking to Billie, wanting to know what she'd seen, what her daddy said before he left. Billie was crying, the TV running under everything like bad water. He went into the house and tried to pick her up, but Curtis Roberts shoved him back. They pushed against each other until Curtis stepped back and pulled out his gun. The other officer rushed over and told him to calm down, there was no call for it. Dee slipped onto the porch and saw Jimmy.

"Jimmy," Dee said. "She's just a little kid."

Jimmy, who knew he wasn't part of no "lower element," Jimmy who Cliff claimed was decent but a product of that time and place. Cliff was always curious about how some men were born deep in the hell of Jim Crow—their daddy a Cyclops of the Klan, or founder of the local White Citizens' Council—but knew it was wrong and dared to be different. Why those men were so few but did exist.

Jimmy looked directly at Dee and walked into the house.

When they were pushing Dee into the back of the car, arresting him for assaulting an officer, he saw Jimmy carrying Billie. She wasn't crying anymore and trying to stay awake, half her hand tucked in her mouth. Dee heard her little baby voice and wanted to call her name, but he didn't want to scare her. He didn't know he wouldn't see his niece for the next thirty years. That he would never get married. That he would never have kids. That his father would die in a few months, his mother have a stroke in a few years. He didn't know how rough it was gonna get because it didn't seem it could get no worse than the one person who ever helped him was lying dead on the ground.

Weeks later Sheila would come over to pay a visit to his momma and he would hear her in the kitchen crying about Curtis Roberts and Dee knew that was the name of one of the men responsible for the death of his brother. Who had handcuffed Cliff instead of taking him to the hospital. And all those men who had helped it happen had blood on their hands.

After Sheila left, his mother made him promise that he say nothing to nobody about it. She would not lose another son, her miracle baby, the only one she had left. She was scared and didn't want more trouble brought on them, or little Billie. Or maybe all her life she had been preparing herself for this kind of pain.

Some nights he would lay awake planning all the ways he could get revenge, and as if she knew, his mother would remind him of his promise and when she couldn't speak she said it with her eyes. He never got justice for Cliff. He just waited for those men to die. Spent the rest of his life trying to slip the weight, to forget that he hadn't made Cliff go to the hospital, that he hadn't spoken up when he had the chance because there was always the chance that worse could happen.

From the police car, he thought he could hear Billie looking for him, wondering where he'd gone. Or maybe she was looking for Cliff, wondering where he was, not knowing her daddy wasn't in this world.

BILLIE

A RETURN TO THE SCENE OF THE CRIME, WHERE HE WAS BORN AND where he died, where at certain times on random days love did not fail even if it could not make them safe.

The dull autumn sun goes behind clouds and Billie zips up her jacket. The harvest is over and the fields are bare. Uncle Dee leans on the hood of the car, smoking, while she goes in to see the new dust and cobwebs as if her stay was already in the distant past.

To get away from the Delta had been good, to let her mind breathe and forget for a little, to be silly, to not be afraid. But this place is in her blood and her blood is in the land and the land is hers.

She sits on the floor and closes her eyes. The house breathes and the bones in the fingers of her left hand ache. "I am not abandoning you," she says. The sun trickles in and fills the cold room, washing up her back.

When King Henry II of England did penance for the murder of Thomas à Becket, the Archbishop of Canterbury, he walked barefoot to Becket's tomb in sackcloth and crown, where he knelt as eighty monks whipped his naked back. But was he sorry that Becket had become a martyr, or that he was responsible for the death of an enemy who had once been a friend?

Outside the icy grass is a blank green, wet in spots. Her boots lie collapsed over one another on the back porch. She traces the yard with her bare feet.

Her uncle is on the front porch when she walks back with her muddy feet stuffed into her boots. "We don't want to be late for dinner at your auntie's. You know how she is," he says as he comes down the steps.

"It's too early to eat." She unlocks the car.

"Girl, that's what you do on Thanksgiving. C'mon, or all the dark meat will be gone."

She doesn't get in, looking at him across the roof of the car. "Did you hear from the prosecutor?"

"Yeah, I spoke to him. He don't sound in a hurry to do nothing." He laughs then meets her eyes. "You sorry you didn't do it?"

A flock of birds rustle from the grass and into the air. "I did what my daddy wanted," she says.

"Amen to that." They climb in and shut the doors.

She stretches her hands on the steering wheel, listening to the wind shake the trees. "I want people to look at Curtis on the street and know what he did. And I want it to be the first thing they remember even after he's dead."

Henry II didn't really want him killed. He'd only ranted about Becket to his knights who went to the cathedral and bludgeoned him to death. But words have blood in them; they can make fate take shape when they pass from a mouth into a heart.

ACKNOWLEDGMENTS

THANK YOU: DENISE SHANNON, FOR YOUR UNSTINTING BRILLIANCE, faith in this book, and generous guidance; Megan Lynch, for seeing what was there before it (fully) was; the Ecco family, whose hard work and amazing support have transformed this story into a tangible thing; Arthur Flowers, for being a force of nature; Danna Anderson, for being you; Christine LeVeaux-Haley, for being a big sister when I had none; Rachel Abelson, Martin De Leon, Andrew Malan Milward, and Steve Barthleme, for being (painfully) early readers; Rhodes College; the University of Houston Honors College; and Sylvester Hoover at the Back in the Day Museum and Johnny B. Thomas at the Emmett Till Historic Intrepid Center, for telling the stories that need to be told and told.

Thank you to Chris and Jules, my ride and dies, my joy.

I am, and continue to be, especially grateful for the tremendous work of David Ridgen and Thomas Moore, Ben Greenberg, Jerry Mitchell, and Stanley Nelson.